****

THE
TWIN
COUSINS

****

A Novel by
Bestselling Author

Jeanetta Britt

Inquiries should be addressed to J. Britt
(brittbooks@msn.com)
Twelve Stones Publishing LLC
P. O. Box 921, Eufaula, AL 36072-0921
www.jbrittbooks.com

Library of Congress Control Number: 2023950770
ISBN: 978-1-7327071-7-7

Printed in the United States
First Edition

Editor: Fairrene Carter-Frost
Cover: Michelle Stimpson

Scriptures from *The Holy Bible*
King James Version

The Lord Knows

©Jeanetta Britt
www.jbrittbooks.com

Of course, the Lord knew
But you had to go through that
To know what you know
Right now

And when you wanted to disappear
Didn't the Lord appear
Even more visible
Than you'd ever seen before?

And in the midst of your pain
His promise still remained
Faithful
And forever true

No matter the trial or test
No matter what others do
"I will never leave
I will never forsake…you!"

Dedication

To...

Larry, Lou, Carolyn, Fairrene, Lizzie Ruth, and Naomie...thank you for a good word at the right time!

All of my Beloved Cousins—on both sides of the family tree—thank you for our strong roots; your loyal, steadfast love; and for the encouraging belly-laughs we've shared together throughout all these many years! Praying the Lord's richest blessings upon you and your families...always!

All of the 'Grand' Cousins—Jaxon, Shiloh, Lyra, and all the rest—I take great delight in seeing you make memories together. Keep the love flowing...always!

Acknowledgments

Readers encourage us to write. Being able to share our gift and calling with others makes our experiences, observations, and testimonies come alive off the page. Thank you to every reader who has ever taken the time to engage with the action-packed, Christian fiction stories that I write. These books are intended to get the word out that Jesus Christ saves, keeps, delivers, heals, and sets free. And I pray that this rousing adventure ('cause life is truly messy) will also lift your hearts and minds to give Him the glory and praise that He—alone—so richly deserves in this mad, mad world!

Thanks, also, to Michelle Stimpson for taking time out of her busy schedule as a national bestselling author, educator, speaker—and patient encourager—to design the perfect cover. And also many thanks to you, Fairrene Carter-Frost, my editor, critic, prayer partner, and long-time friend for never pulling any punches and for always saying exactly what you see. It is of immense value to me and the quality of these narratives.

Now, it's my hope that you'll enjoy the journey—the mystery and the madness. Buckle up…it's a wildly inspiring ride!

****

"Fear them not therefore: for there is nothing covered,
that shall not be revealed; and hid, that shall not be known."
~Matthew 10:26

PROLOGUE

"'Mary Mack, Mack, Mack! All dressed in black, black, black! With silver buttons, buttons, buttons! All down her back, back, back—'"

"Stop it, Hope! You messed up again. You're always messing up. You've got to clap right!"

"Okay, Joy…but I'm doing my best—"

"Well, your best isn't good enough! 'Cause if you're gonna be *my* twin cousin, Hope, you've gotta be as good as me. And I'm the pretty one, remember? Everyone says so—"

"Oh, alright, Joy. I'm sorry. I will. I'll try harder."

CHAPTER 1

It was a bright, breezy day in April the first time Nurse Joy Greene strutted up to the front door at 2200 Bird of Paradise Road. The heaviness of winter was giving way to the promise of spring, and there was not a cloud in the crystal blue sky. A faint whiff of sweetness permeated the morning air, which was provided by the majestic magnolias that bordered the estate. As was her practice, Nurse Greene had arrived for her appointment promptly at 10 a.m. Being a highly-skilled geriatric and hospice nurse, she was very conscientious in her duties and excellent in her manner. She'd also mastered the knack of separating the pain of her patients from her own personal pleasures, and that single attribute had elevated her head-and-shoulders above her peers. It was the key to her growing success in her field. She always wore her agency's colors on her first home visit—a bright and airy canary yellow skimmer with sensible tan loafers—and today was no exception. She took a deep breath, inhaled her new surroundings, and rang the doorbell. *But who in their right mind would build a dream home like this out here in these sticks? Humph!*

While she waited, Joy removed her custom-designed sunglasses, flipped back her dark, flowing curls, and allowed the sunshine to kiss her caramel face. She was all smiles inside because her day had been uniquely interesting so far. Unlike the thick traffic she had to contend with in Metro Atlanta, Joy had enjoyed a quiet ride on Georgia's curvy backroads that were littered with little more than tall pines and crooked mailboxes scattered every few hundred feet. The abandoned farmhouses, idle tractors, and broken-down vehicles that she encountered along the way may have represented the trail of someone else's broken dreams, but certainly not her own. No, on the contrary, her heart was beaming with pride because her unique skill-set afforded her the opportunity to ply her trade with any high-dollar agency in the world. But it was her own personal choice to stay close to the home she'd grown to love in Lawrenceville, Georgia, a northern-tier suburb of Atlanta. *And I'm able to stash away lots o' cheese while doing things my way...ha!*

When a man finally answered the door, his striking good looks shook Joy's nerves to the core. Under his face mask and haggard expression stood a very handsome man. He was tall, muscular, with wavy, dark hair and skin the color of whipped milk chocolate. And behind that mask was an exceptional pair of deep, hazel eyes. *Whoa! What a hunk! He must certainly have an in-home gym tucked away in this mansion.* Her next reaction was to wish she'd worn something more revealing to show off her own curves; but in the meantime, she was very happy her face mask was concealing her complete awe and utter amazement. "Uhh—" Joy attempted a swift recovery. "Good morning, sir...are you Mr. Sterling?"

"Yes, I am," the man replied, raising his smooth, dark brows. "How may I help you?"

The sound of his rich baritone sent shockwaves through Joy's heart; it did a giant flip-flop and skipped several beats. *This man is absolutely F-ine...Rich...and hid out here in these backwoods with a sick wife...and, now, with little ole me? Yes, indeed, this is going to be one, very interesting assignment.* "Uhh...I'm Joy...Joy Greene," she finally responded to his quizzical looks with an uncharacteristic stutter. "I'm with the Hightower Medical Agency, Inc. I'm your...Hospice Nurse," she said, while awkwardly handing him a full packet of her agency's information. Her business card, which included her name and private cell number, topped the stack. Her agency was a renowned concierge medical practice that catered to a wealthy clientele in need of discreet and specialized in-home care for their loved ones.

"Yes. Welcome. I'm Sam...Sam Sterling," the man said expectantly while opening the storm door to accept the packet and allow Joy to enter his impressive home. It was a sprawling split-level mansion, set on nearly ten acres of expertly manicured grounds. It boasted of eight bedrooms, ten full baths, and every conceivable amenity, including a media room; a lavish, glass-enclosed swimming pool; and, of course, an in-home gym.

"You can call me Nurse Greene...Nurse Joy...or just Joy...if you prefer—"

"Come in. Come on in," Sam Sterling invited. He showed Joy into the living room and cleared a space on the enameled side table for her briefcase. "Can I get you anything...to drink or eat," he asked, fumbling awkwardly with the stack of papers before setting them atop her briefcase.

"No, thank you." Joy's voice had regained its composure, and it offered him a pretty smile. "I'm fine. Just fine."

"Would you like to freshen up before meeting my wife...your patient?"

"Thank you," Joy said sweetly. "I always like to wash up before going into a patient's room. I'll be right out," she said after being directed to the perfectly-appointed full bath on the first floor. When she returned, she was glad to see Sam Sterling waiting there to escort her upstairs.

"Baby?" Sam lowered his mask and his baritone when they reached his wife's bedroom. His voice was full of love notes as he spoke quietly to her. "You awake, sweetie? I've got somebody I want you to meet—"

"Huh?" His wife rolled over groggily; she was in obvious pain. "Yes, babe, I'm awake—"

"Good." Sam raised a smile and led Joy closer to the bed. "Baby, this is...Nurse Greene. She's here to help you feel better. Nurse Greene, this is my lovely, warrior-queen wife, Sam...Samantha Sterling," Sam said, heralding her name with great pride.

3

"Oh-h? I don't know about all that." Samantha's voice squeaked. "But it does sound good coming from the sweet lips of my handsome, warrior-king husband."

"Hello." Joy blushed under her mask because now having seen him full faced, she was in complete agreement. Sam Sterling was the full package. *This man is absolutely...The One!!*

"Come closer," Samantha invited with the wave of a weak hand. "Come."

"Sure." Joy cast a caring glance in Sam's direction and stepped closer to his wife's hospice bed. "It's very good to meet you, Mrs. Sterling," she said in her efficient, caretaker tone. "I'm here to make you more comfortable and to help you get better, and I'm sure we'll get along famously."

Samantha forced herself to one side for a closer look at Nurse Greene. "You're a very pretty, young girl," she said, although the two of them were very close in age—mid-thirties. Samantha Sterling had been a very pretty girl, too. However, the ravages of her disease—pronounced by hair thinning and rapid weight loss—had left her comparatively small and weak; and her once brilliantly flawless cocoa complexion was now very pale and sallow.

"Please excuse me, Mr. Sterling...Mrs. Sterling—" an older woman said as she politely tapped on the bedroom door. She was outfitted in a white smock, and her short, salt-and-pepper wig was pulled down neatly over her ears.

"Oh, yes, Mrs. Barnes," Sam said, greeting her warmly. "This is Nurse Joy Greene...the medical professional we've been expecting."

"Yes, sir." The portly woman nodded politely and shifted her weight to her left hip to gain a better view of the newcomer.

"Nurse Greene, I'd like you to meet Mrs. Lily Barnes. She's our treasured housekeeper, and she's been with us for many years. Don't know what we would do without her."

"Very nice to meet you, Mrs. Barnes," Joy said, intentionally on her best behavior.

"Likewise," Mrs. Barnes replied rather skeptically, "I'm sure."

"Mrs. Barnes, please get Nurse Greene's guestroom ready on this floor, and we'll be dining at 6 p.m."

"Yes, of course, Mr. Sterling," Mrs. Barnes said with respectful deference, although she was at least 20 years his senior. Her white, rubber-soled shoes emitted a noticeable squeak as she tromped away to handle her household duties. The sound was a constant reminder to the Sterlings that they were in very caring and very capable hands.

"I assume everyone in the house has been fully vaccinated against the Covid virus." Joy's voice buzzed closely into Sam's ear. "I noticed Mrs. Barnes was not wearing a mask."

"Of course," Sam replied. "Anyone who comes near the house at any time is fully checked, and Mrs. Barnes lives here. She goes out very infrequently. We have our necessities delivered, and she is very thorough about cleaning and sanitizing all items that we receive."

"Well, that's good news," Joy said, "and, of course, I'm fully vaccinated, as well. It's just that we can't be too careful with Mrs. Sterling in her delicate condition—"

"I fully agree." Sam offered her a crisp nod and returned his full attention back to his beloved wife. "Baby, I'll get Nurse Greene a chair," he said, "and let you two, lovely ladies have a pleasant visit while I go downstairs to handle some business calls."

"Thank you," Joy said as Sam brought over a comfortable side chair and excused himself to allow the ladies to talk.

"You are very young," Samantha Sterling wheezed, shooting straight to the point as was her style. She pressed her bed's remote button to slightly elevate her head for better breathing and for a better view of this new female presence invading her home. "You must've worked very hard to get so far so fast."

"Yes, I did. I went straight through from being an undergraduate at Fisk to graduate school at Tuskegee to become a specialized Registered Nurse, and I've had lots of subsequent training and good practice ever since…so I'm really not that young. I'm nearly 36."

"Me, too." Samantha squirmed, mourning the loss of her own beauty compared to that of her contemporary. "Nearly 37."

"So, how can I make you feel more comfortable while I'm here, Mrs. Sterling?" Joy's voice turned clinical. "You name it."

"No. Please…call me Samantha…my husband is the only one who ever calls me Sam…since that could get rather confusing—" She attempted a chuckle that morphed into a cough.

"Thanks," Joy said, passing her a wad of tissues. "And you can call me Joy…if you wish—"

"J-o-y?" Samantha's voice forced a brave smile. "Sure! That's exactly what we need around here—"

"So, then…what can I do to make you more comfortable, Samantha?"

"Well, Joy, my sweet husband has been giving me my wash offs, but I'd rather a woman…you know…help me in the bathroom, so I can get a proper shower…wash my hair and such. Sam is willing, but I'm his wife. I don't really want him to see me…as a patient—"

"I understand perfectly." Joy gently patted her new patient's hand and removed her own mask. "And that will be no problem at all. I'll be with you around the clock, five days a week; and we'll take it one step at a time. Okay?"

"Thank you." Samantha breathed a noticeable sigh of relief and refocused her tired eyes to size-up Nurse Joy Greene. "Yes, indeed, you really are a very pretty girl…and it'll be so good to have another woman in the house…you know, closer to my own age."

CHAPTER 2

The next morning, bright and early, Dr. Harvey Wallace arrived at the Sterling's elegant residence on Bird of Paradise Road. He was a hunched-over man in his fifties with greying temples and insightful blue eyes. He was considered the guru of the doctors in his field. He had been Samantha's doctor when she'd been diagnosed, and he'd overseen her earlier radiation and chemo treatments at the Stringer Memorial Cancer Center in Atlanta—one of the most renowned, state-of-the-art facilities of its kind. It ranked right up there with MD Anderson in Houston, but its location was more accessible to the Sterlings.

Dr. Wallace didn't usually make house calls, but he'd made an exception in Samantha's case. Given the gene-type of her cancer, he thought a medical breakthrough in her case might be possible. And if so, a successful treatment plan in her case could be transferrable to other similar patients. It was his practice to make his bi-weekly visits to evaluate Samantha's progress on Mondays, but he wanted to allow the new nurse to get settled-in before he arrived. Dr. Wallace was greeted warmly by Mrs. Barnes at the front door, and she ushered him in to see Sam who was busily working in his home office.

"Good morning, Sam," the doctor said heartily. "How are you?"

"I'm well, doctor," Sam replied. "And I'm glad you made it through our little rainstorm."

"No problem. I like to keep my schedule as closely as possible in order to monitor our beautiful patient." The doctor offered him a tired smile. "How's Samantha been doing since my last visit?"

"She's been more upbeat than usual," Sam said. "And that's great. I think the idea of having a new, live-in nurse appeals to her. And as it turns out, they're very close in age."

"Well, that's good. Where's our new nurse?"

"Her name is Nurse Joy Greene," Sam said. "And she's upstairs with Samantha—"

"Oh, I'm well aware of who she is," Dr. Wallace explained. "Her credentials preceded her. Her agency sent them to my office for review and approval before we offered her the assignment."

"That's good to know." Sam nodded. "So, are you ready to go upstairs and see the ladies?"

"Just let me wash-up down here first, and I'll be right with you," the doctor said, securing his face mask.

When the two men entered the upstairs bedroom, Nurse Greene was administering a breathing treatment and checking Samantha's vital signs with a blood pressure monitor. She quickly stopped the process when the two men entered the room.

"Oh, good morning," Joy said brightly. "And you must be Dr. Wallace?" She smiled, making special note of his medical bag.

"Yes, I am," Dr. Wallace said, "and I'm very pleased that you're here to attend to Mrs. Sterling's needs. And if I may say so, you are quite a lovely young lady...nearly as beautiful as my patient, here. But I would ask that you always wear your face mask when you're in her room—"

"Oh, I'm so sorry, doctor, I—"

"No need to apologize; I understand." The doctor raised his hand in dismissal. "Thankfully, we're on the tail-end of this pandemic, and you're a valued member of the household. But since I'm planning to administer a new drug in Mrs. Sterling's case that may seriously compromise her immune system, I want all of us to maintain strict Covid protocols from this point forward to ensure my patient's safety. Agreed?"

"Certainly, doctor, I understand," Joy said crisply, "and I agree."

"Great! I knew I could count on you," Dr. Wallace said, turning to Sam. "And as I was saying to Mr. Sterling downstairs, I reviewed your credentials, Nurse Greene, before you accepted this assignment; and they are stellar."

"Why, thank you, doctor," Joy said, blushing appropriately. She was delighted that Sam was being apprised of her respected reputation in the medical community—without it having to come from her own lips.

"And you possess the perfect skill-set for this assignment, Nurse Greene," the doctor continued, "and I will be counting on you heavily to ensure that things go well with Mrs. Sterling—"

"Mrs. Sterling?!? Well, that would be Samantha to you, Doc," his patient said in a minor fit of coughing, "or are you planning to keep talking about me like I'm not in the room, huh? But I, for one, think we've been working together far too long to get me well for us to be so formal. Now, don't you?"

"For sure!" The doctor chuckled. He was always encouraged by Samantha's plucky attitude and joyful spirit despite the seriousness of her chronic illness. "We are certainly all working as a team to keep Samantha as comfortable as possible," he said. "And I've been working on a new course of treatment that will strengthen you and improve your prognosis—"

"Now, that's what I'm talking about!" Samantha said, laying aside her breathing apparatus so she could speak more freely. "I want to get stronger, and I expect to get stronger. Sam and I have too many plans and too many wonderful things left to do…even if I have to do some of them from this bed for a little while—"

"I was saying to Nurse Greene, Samantha, after evaluating your last labs, I'm starting you on the new drug protocol this week," Dr. Wallace said. "It has to be administered intravenously, and Nurse Greene is just the right person to do the job. But while we're trying this new cocktail, I need for everyone around you to wear their face masks. We want to be sure that you are kept safe while your immune system is being challenged. Especially you, Nurse Greene, because as I understand it, you'll be going back and forth to Metro Atlanta on the weekends."

"Yes, sir." Joy pursed her lips behind her face mask. "I'm off on Fridays and Saturdays."

"And Sam, I know you make it a practice to work from home, but on those rare occasions when you must go to outside meetings, it might be wise for you to wear a mask, as well."

"I understand, doctor, and that's no problem," Sam said. "There's nothing more important in this world than keeping my girl safe."

"Aww, babe!" Samantha cooed.

"Okay, Nurse Greene, let's go downstairs and review your new orders…and give these two love birds some privacy."

"Of course," Joy said, turning her attentions to Sam in an attempt to ingratiate herself to the handsome man-of-the-house. "That is, if it's alright with you, Mr. Sterling—"

"Huh? Yes, of course," Sam said, plastering her with a puzzled look. "My wife and I will be perfectly fine here together…but we really do appreciate both of you."

"Come on, Nurse Greene," the doctor said, prodding her along. "We have some very important work to do."

When the medical professionals had left the room, Samantha used the remote to lower her bed. "I know we've got mountains to climb, baby." She smiled weakly at her husband. "But if it's okay with you, I'm gonna start with a little nap—"

Sam pulled up a chair near her bedside. "And I'm gonna sit right here with you until you fall asleep." He held her thin hand and caressed it gently.

"That's so sweet of you, husband…so very, very sweet—"

As Samantha drifted off into a drug-induced haze, Sam rehearsed their precious memories. *Oh, how I remember the making of us,*

Samantha...like it was yesterday. He mused. *We've got history, Sweet Baby. Us...together...always...against the world!*

****

You and I met the first week of freshman year at our beloved Hampton University: "Our home by the sea!" Your maiden name was Starke, and we met in that dreaded, long registration line for which HBCUs are famous. And besides sharing the S through T line with the rest of the freshman "Littles"—all of us eagerly longing to be accepted as full-fledged Pirates—I was from Newark, New Jersey, and you from Buffalo, New York; and this was our first forage below the Mason-Dixon line.

"What're they making in there...flapjacks or something?" I heard you spout under your breath, and I laughed at your quirky comment. I laughed, and you turned around and smiled at me. And there you were...long, lanky, and lovely with a brilliant sense of humor. Your smile was so shimmering, so open, so pure; it made me feel weak in the knees. And just like that, I knew. I could look at that smile for the rest of my life and never tire of it. And just like that, the two of us became inseparable. We had a four-year courtship, and we were married the day after graduation at the courthouse. It wasn't fancy...we didn't want fancy...we wanted true and forever. We had a plan, you and I, and we wanted to work it...together.

We agreed that I would go on to grad school at UCLA and Cal Tech to become an engineer. And, Samantha, it was you who insisted on taking a job...any job...to support us. But by a brilliant stroke of good fortune, you got the job as Assistant to the Dean of Student Affairs at the university. And I can remember that day you came home...so excited. You'd just attended a chapel service on campus, and you came through the door of our tiny apartment shouting, "Sam! Sam! You've just got to come with me. I've heard the most astonishing news...Jesus Christ is very much alive...and, baby, He wants to help us live, too!" From that time forward, my love, you and I were hooked. I went to the next chapel meeting, and we both got saved on the spot. We even got baptized together. It was a glorious time, and it was a turning point in our lives. It gave true purpose and meaning to the plans that we'd been making.

We really wanted children, you and I...but it wasn't in God's plan for us. Your uterus was overrun by fibroids and conception was impossible...a bad case of fourth-stage endometriosis the doctors called it. We were so very disappointed. I remember us crying in each other's arms one whole night...but it couldn't break us. Our bond of love is too strong to be broken by disappointment of any kind. In fact, I think it made us stronger...closer to the Lord...closer to each other. It gave us a greater desire to fulfil the purpose He had for our lives. I guess that's why, shortly after that devastating news, we felt led to move down here to the Atlanta area...and for me to finally start my own business. We believed the business would be our baby, and we would nurture it...together.

When I started Sterling Engineering, Inc., I was really blessed to be able to assemble a network of some of the most brilliant minds in the field...on a global scale...to develop some of the most lucrative and innovative projects, worldwide. I'd met most of these smart knuckleheads during my stent at Hampton, UCLA and Cal Tech, but the rest of our young, hungry partners just followed the breadcrumbs to our door.

The sophisticated proprietary software that we've been able to develop has allowed us to have virtual meetings that are highly interactive and very successful...and just in the nick of time, too. Our consortium can meet remotely; distribute assignments; and then, each individual company can handle their piece of the design and construction puzzle. Me and my guys, or one of the other firms, can compile the final results and add the necessary finishing touches for a successful project. That's our market niche, and it's been working mighty good for us, particularly, through this pandemic. Our companies have succeeded where others have failed. And it's also fixed it so I rarely have to travel. And that's fine by me because, Samantha, I cherish our time together. And when I do have to travel, I can make it targeted and brief.

And, yes, I can remember the day after our business finally picked up, and I was able to come home and say, "Samantha Sterling, you're officially retired! You've worked long enough to keep us afloat, and it's time for you to take it easy!" Baby, you took the news somewhat reluctantly, but as always, you followed my lead. And with your usual warm smile and sassy way, you said, "Well, buddy, you've got yourself a deal!"

And when we moved down here to Sandywood, we decided to build our dream home and fellowship under Pastor Jamie's leadership. But you didn't just come into your big, brand-new mansion and sit down. Nope! You listened to all of his sermons. You joined me in prayer and fasting. And then, you got this bright idea to start the first-ever, free food pantry at the church. And it was a hit from the start! That's my girl!

I'm so proud of you, Samantha. You not only did that, but you also volunteer and serve on the board of our local orphanage where you actually advocate in the court system for these precious, little children. We couldn't have our own, but you give voice to these children's pain and their special needs...as only you can. You have a heart as big as Texas, my love, and you were going at it great guns...until...until that awful day about a year ago when you could no longer stand on your own two feet. Sure, you'd been having stomach trouble for a while...but...but who could've imagined...who could've ever fathomed...that your diagnosis would go from simple gastritis...to pancreatic cancer—

Quietly, Sam kissed his wife's fragile hand and tucked it beneath her warm covers. "Sleep well, my sweet baby," he whispered. Rising from his chair, he fell to his knees at her bedside. "Dear Lord, this sickness has taken her down, but I pray...please, Lord...don't let it take her out!" he said softly. "Oh, my sweet baby, I love you so very much, and we've come so far together...please...please don't leave me...don't ever, ever leave me—" Finally, Sam gave in to his own tortured tears.

CHAPTER 3

"Well, ladies, I'm gonna have to leave it with you," Sam Sterling said the next evening after dinner. "I've really got some pressing assignments to finish in my office. Excellent meal as always, Mrs. Barnes—"

"Thank you, Mr. Sterling," Mrs. Barnes replied with a kind nod as she plated her fork and set her napkin aside.

"Oh, Sam," Joy called after him in a velvety voice, "now, don't you work too hard—" To which, he offered no reply.

"Who're your people, anyhow, Nurse Greene?" Mrs. Barnes scowled. It had not escaped her notice that Joy only had eyes for Sam throughout dinner. And earlier in the day, she'd spied her at the pool, wearing nothing but a skimpy bikini at a time when she knew Sam would be in his private office, which just so happened to overlook the pool. She'd watched Joy as she completed her expert laps, and then posed her long, sleek, shimmering legs in a lounge chair like a centerfold model in a girlie magazine. Mrs. Barnes had been pretty sure that the exhibition was for Sam's benefit, and she intended to get to the heart of the matter very quickly.

"My people?" Joy pursed her lips. "What on earth do you mean, ma'am?"

"I mean…how were you raised, young lady? Did you have a church home?"

"Of course, I did—"

"Then I expect you to act like it while you're under this roof!" Mrs. Barnes said, evil-eyeing the exposed cleavage under Joy's sheer, white blouse. "Mr. & Mrs. Sterling are good, God-fearing people, and I don't want no messy business up in here while you're in this house. Do you understand me?"

"No, ma'am, I'm sure I don't have a clue." Joy's voice frosted over as though she were speaking to a mere servant. "Now, if you'll excuse me, *Miz* Barnes, I'll take Samantha her dinner—"

Oh, no, you will not!" Mrs. Barnes blared. "You did it yesterday, and I let it pass; but I'll be the one taking Mrs. Sterling her dinner." Mrs. Barnes pushed back from the table and stood defiantly with her arms clamped tightly across her chest. "In fact, I have Mr. Sterling's permission to take her all of her meals from now on. Mrs. Sterling doesn't like for her husband to do it because…sometimes…well, sometimes she has trouble holding her fork and finding her mouth. And, besides, she'd much rather spend time with her husband talking, and planning, and laughing, and such. And you don't need to deliver her meals 'cause she don't need you reminding her of her illness every moment of the day." Mrs. Barnes flapped around the table like a mother hen. "She needs to see as many different people as possible. She needs to be around the people who love her, Nurse Greene—"

"Oh, you can call me Joy—"

"Oh, I know what I can call you, *Nurse Greene*…but you'd better stay in your place while you're in this house!" Mrs. Barnes made a brisk exit to the kitchen, leaving Joy standing there flatfooted and alone.

Did I go to church? Why, yes, you old crow! Joy's childhood memories flashed across her mind like they were on the big screen. *Of course, I went to our church…every Sunday…like clockwork. My folks' lives revolved around Greater Harvest Christian Church of Kansas City, Missouri. And my family history…well…okay…it is a wee-bit complicated—*

****

Well, as the story goes, the Whyte twins—Faith and Grace—met and married the Greene twins—James and John—at Greater Harvest

Christian Church of Kansas City, Missouri. The Whyte and Greene families had been friends and faithful churchgoers for decades. Since the parents of the Whyte twins had birthed their two daughters late in life, they'd been over the moon with the opportunity to have children of their own. And since they'd attributed their long-awaited blessing to God's goodness, they gave their twin girls very special names— Faith and Grace. Both Faith and Grace grew up to be very pretty girls. They were both kissed with smooth, caramel skin, and they both took special pains with their hair, which was kinky and tight.

The Greene family, on the other hand, already had an older son, Jude. And Jude was often heard to say, "Yeah, I was the oldest, alright, but as soon as those twin boys came along, I got pushed to the back…way to the back. But no worries; I've learned to fend for myself!" Since the Greenes had already decided to name each of their sons after their favorite books in the Bible, their twin boys were christened—James and John. The twins were the center of attention everywhere they went, and their parents basked in the limelight. The boys grew up to bear a strong resemblance to each other—tall, nut-brown, handsome, and with coal-black, wavy hair.

"Well, growing up so closely in this church, I guess it was only destiny that them Whyte twins and Greene twins would meet and marry one another," Pastor J. R. Jones was often heard to say, even from the pulpit. And so, it was—James and Faith; John and Grace— inevitably met, courted, and fell in love at Greater Harvest Christian Church. Their combined wedding ceremony had been the talk of the town, and the framed pictures that lined each of their mantles were a thing of beauty. And even after their nuptials, the twin couples— James and Faith Greene; John and Grace Greene—remained very close. They were so close, in fact, they lived just one street over from each other—James and Faith lived on 71st Street; and John and Grace lived on 71st Terrace, between Prospect and The Paseo near Swope Park.

Before long, the twin sisters—Faith and Grace—became pregnant at the same time. It was a miraculous coincidence in their eyes. And when Faith and Grace found out they were both having girls, the two couples conjured up a plan. Whichever of the girls would be born first, they agreed to name her *Hope*; and the second arrival would be named, *Joy*. The naming pact was a closely-held family secret, and both couples awaited the births with great expectation.

In due course, Faith and Grace found themselves in the same hospital, on the same day, and they were all very excited. When Faith gave birth first, her husband, James, ran to the other end of the corridor to inform his brother, John, that they'd named their daughter—Hope—as they'd all agreed. And when Grace and John's baby girl greeted the world, she was given the agreed-upon name—Joy. For the couples had covenanted that when these two cousins were seen together—which would be most often—people would be forced to say, "Here comes...Hope and Joy!" The baby girls were born thirty minutes apart, well and healthy; and both families were elated. And when Hope and Joy came of age, the two cousins were also entrusted with the family's secret naming pact.

From that point on, Hope and Joy were brought up more like sisters than cousins—twin sisters, in fact. When you saw one, you saw the other. They attended the same schools, the same church. They were members of the same clubs and social groups. They even had the same piano teacher, but Joy was a natural, and she always tried to outshine her cousin, Hope. They even wore matching outfits—even though they were built quite differently.

And it was the notable difference in their physical makeup that most people immediately observed. Joy had inherited her mother's smooth, caramel skin and her dad's dark, wavy hair. She was tall and stately with fine features and a slender face that got much attention. Even as a young child, Joy was self-assured, self-centered, and strong-willed, which gave her a mystique that many adults admired.

18

JEANETTA BRITT

Her cousin, Hope, on the other hand, had inherited her daddy's nut-brown skin, and her mother's hair, which was kinky and tight. Hope was also short and chunky with a dimple in her left cheek and a pair of big, brown eyes that nearly dwarfed her other features. And unlike her feisty cousin, Hope had a quiet, sensitive, and compassionate nature—the kind of traits that largely go unnoticed. Nonetheless, the two cousins were inseparable, and their parents encouraged and promoted their closeness. Over the years, Hope and Joy Greene grew into an incomparable duo. In all things academic, they were a force to be reckoned with. And despite their stark physical differences, the people who knew and loved them had quickly dubbed them—*The Twin Cousins*—and the name stuck.

Yup, we were joined at the hip back then...even before we were born...thanks to our doting parents. Joy smirked at the recollection and polished off her glass of iced tea while sitting alone at the empty dining room table. *Yup...there's no denying it...we are, in fact, "The Twin Cousins"! But, I've turned out to be smart and pretty...while Hope...poor, sweet Hope...well, she's just pretty weak. She might've been born a few minutes before me, but I'm the princess, and she's the frog...and such is life. Ha!*

CHAPTER 4

The next night at dinner, Joy pushed away her lovingly prepared plate of baked chicken and wild rice with a fine cabbage medley. The dining room table, which had been set for two, was warmed under the soft glow of the chandelier that accentuated the beauty of the simple place settings. However, the great meal and lovely surroundings were lost on Joy. She'd dressed for the occasion in an eye-popping, red silk sundress that was as stunning as it was skimpy, and she was miffed. Joy flicked back her dark curls, folded her arms across her exposed bosom, and squeezed out scalding words between clenched teeth. "Where is Sam, Mrs. Barnes? Why isn't he here for dinner?"

"Well, not that it's any of yo' business," Mrs. Barnes snipped back, "but Mr. Sterling fasts on Thursdays and has Bible Study with his wife instead of the evening meal—"

"Fasting? Why?" Joy's lips plumped peevishly. "Sam's not the least bit overweight—"

"Pastor Jamie encourages us to fast regularly...not simply to deny ourselves food or worldly pleasures, but to take the time to feed on God's word," Mrs. Barnes said, directing her words and prickly stare at Joy's bosom. "And to ward off any and all...distractions."

"Is that so—"

"And if you stay around here for more than a week, Nurse Greene, you'll come to understand the comings and goings of this household." Mrs. Barnes allowed her fork to drop nosily onto her plate. "That is if you get to stay—"

"Of course, I'll get to stay," Joy snipped. "Samantha's doctor has ordered some specialized treatments that require my expert attention—"

"So…you told me you went to church every Sunday with your family." Mrs. Barnes shifted the subject and resumed her meal. "Do you still keep in touch…with your family, I mean?"

"Well, if you must know, Miz Barnes, my parents are both deceased…tragic car accident five years ago." Joy stiffened. "Not something I really like to talk about…but I do have a cousin who still lives in Kansas City. Her parents live there, too…although I understand they're both in failing health. She has to keep a close watch on them. And my daddy's other brother, Uncle Jude, lives in the Atlanta area…but our paths never seem to cross…both too busy, I guess—"

"Does your Uncle Jude have children?"

"No, he never married. My cousin and I are the only two children in our family."

Well, you're blessed." Mrs. Barnes granted. "My family is all gone. I guess Mr. & Mrs. Sterling are like the son and daughter I never had. I lost my husband, too, you see…and it's a very lonely business—"

"Yes, I can clearly see that." *You ole prude!* "But you needn't worry; that'll never happen to me."

"Well, let's pray not." Mrs. Barnes raised her brows. "But counting yo' chickens before they hatch is a sure-fire way to get yo' feelings hurt. People let you down; Jesus never will. Pastor Jamie tells us that every Sunday—"

"Well, people may intend to let you down." Joy bristled. "But if you're smart enough, you can get people to do just about anything you please—"

"Oh, yeah…well, good luck with that—"

"Oh, no, it's not luck. It's skill." Joy snickered under her breath. *But what would you know about that, Miz Lily Barnes? You're the epitome of an 'average' woman…emptying bedpans and slaving over a hot stove…while I, on the other hand, am a successful, professional woman. And, yes, ma'am, being both pretty and smart like me…I can have anything I want!*

"Did you say something?"

"Oh, no…nothing." Joy giggled into her napkin. "But who is this, Pastor Jamie? I heard Sam…and Samantha…talking about him—"

"Oh, he's our young minister…Pastor Jamie Ridley. They moved down to these parts from up north somewhere. He's a li'l…hippie-fied…I guess you'd say…long, blonde, shaggy hair. But him and his li'l red-headed wife, Melissa, are the heartbeat of Sandywood Bible Fellowship—

"So, you've got a white pastor?"

"Sho! We got white members, too. We're what you'd call an interracial church—"

"I'm surprised that would go over down here—"

"Pastor Jamie can handle it. He rarely sugarcoats thangs like we're known to do down here in the south. And his way is growing on us. He's a straightshooter, and the unvarnished truth from the Bible is exactly what we all need. He believes the Lord's way is right, and they came to us teaching, preaching, and practicing the simple Gospel message—"

"Which is?"

"Follow Jesus Christ, and love one another! And in that way, color and race don't really enter into the picture—"

"Oh, I see—"

"And that's why we've got a real active church, too. We've got our hands in some o' everything in this community. Pastor Jamie says the multitudes flocked to Jesus…even into hot deserts, high mountains, and seashores…'cause they knew He'd have compassion on them and care for them. And if people are going to flock to Jesus today, they've gotta first see that His church cares about them…not just in word, but in deed. Jesus' life proved that people will flock to wherever they're being fed the bread of life. You know…truth, love, respect, comfort, and care. And, as a result, some might even get saved—"

"Well, thank you very much for that mini-sermon, Miz Barnes," Joy said, humoring her enthusiasm and mining for as much information as she could get on Sam Sterling's interests. Afterall, a big-game hunter needs to know everything she can about her prey. "So, I'd imagine Sam serves on the leadership team. Right?"

"Of course, he does, and he's a very influential member, too. Sam is a very generous man, a very caring man, and he carries a lot of weight in this county...but so does Mrs. Sterling," Mrs. Barnes said proudly. "In fact, she was the one who came up with the idea to start-up our church's first, free food pantry—"

"Is that right—"

"Yeah, and Pastor Jamie ain't like some preachers who'll shoot down your ideas. He doesn't see the talents and gifts of the congregation as a threat to his authority, or treat folk like they tryna show off...or even worse, like they tryna show him up. Naw, Pastor Jamie's not like that at all—"

"Really?"

"No, he's as quick to praise the good works of others as he is to pointing out the stumbling blocks that might be in their way. He embraces the move of the Spirit in the hearts and lives of his fellow saints, so that we can sow into the lives of people...both inside and outside the church's walls. Yup, he's real open to new ideas, especially the ones that're gonna help somebody."

"So, you think that's why Samantha started the free food pantry?"

"Sho! And that free food pantry is helping a lot of people in Sandywood and Armstrong County, too, especially during this pandemic. You can believe me on that—"

"So, does this fantastic pastor of yours have any children?"

"Yeah, Pastor and Melissa, they've got themselves a pair o' twin boys. They're cute as a button, but baddd. The whole congregation's gotta watch out for them li'l towheaded buggers…but we loves 'em dearly.

"Well, since Sam…and Samantha…are so involved in the church, I might consider attending as well—"

"Well, you just do that. Everybody's welcome." Mrs. Barnes lowered her fork and set her knife across it. "But do keep in mind, Nurse Greene, you won't be able to go to first service with Mr. Sterling…and me. No, ma'am! You've gotta stay here and watch over Mrs. Sterling while we're gone. But our church does offer a second service every Sunday. That is, if you're so inclined—"

"Like I said, Miz Barnes, I'll think about it." Joy flung her napkin into her chair and stormed away from the dining table, leaving her lovely dinner untouched.

CHAPTER 5

"So, then, what shall we do today, my love?" Sam curled up next to Samantha in her hospice bed. He and Samantha had a standing date to always be together on Fridays and Saturdays. There'd be no Nurse Greene, no orders, no treatments, no needles for two whole days, and they were eagerly looking forward to sharing the respite together.

"I don't know," Samantha said, as she cast her eyes upon her beloved. "What do you suggest?"

"Well, I've checked the weather, and it's supposed to be a bright, sunny day," Sam said eagerly. "And I'm tired of just looking out of my office window onto our beautiful pool. What if I were to escort you poolside, and we have our lunch served out there."

"Oh, that sounds splendid…but…I don't know if I can manage the stairs—"

"Who said anything about you managing the stairs?" Sam smiled broadly. "We'll use the elevator. That's why I had it installed, and I'll bring your chariot around and whisk you to the pool myself. What kind of cheap date do you take me for?"

"Sam, you're so silly!" Samantha's happy laughter mixed with a subtle wheeze. "Then, I gladly accept your invitation, kind sir, and I'll wear something befitting the grand occasion—"

"Well, you do just that. And I'll call Mrs. Barnes to assist you, and I'll be awaiting your call to swing your chariot around—"

"I can't wait!" Samantha smiled; and it was the same smile that had made Sam weak in the knees the first day he'd ever laid eyes on her.

"Ahh, this is so lovely." Samantha sighed when Sam parked her wheelchair at the white wicker table under their glass-enclosed pool.

The water was bright blue and sparkling, setting the tone for a very relaxing afternoon. "Spring is really here," Samantha said, admiring the yellow daffodils that bordered the walkway. "I'm glad I planted those bulbs when we moved here."

"Yes, they're still quite beautiful…just like you." Sam's eyes embraced her. "And I asked Mrs. Barnes to bring our lunch any time she chooses so we can just take our time and enjoy. But I see she's left us some snacks to munch on in the meantime." There was a veggie tray; chips and dips; iced tea; lemonade; and freshly-baked chocolate chip cookies. Samantha's favorite water bottle had also been placed there since she insisted on taking it everywhere. It was covered with butterflies in assorted, brilliant colors. She'd ordered it special because she'd said, "It reminds me that we're all born caterpillars, but God can transform us into butterflies…if we'll just let Him."

"Mrs. Barnes is always so thoughtful—"

"Yes, she is," Sam said, "she's like the mother I lost—"

"Does that still bother you?" Samantha cooed. "I know it used to lay heavy on your heart—"

"No," Sam reassured his wife, "not anymore…thanks to you. You've helped me see that death is a line we can't cross, and I have a brighter outlook now—"

"I guess losing both of my parents was a little different for me, Sam," Samantha said sweetly. "I grew up in a happy home…only child. And since they both died before I even met you, I had a longer time to process it and to adjust."

"True." Sam nodded. And as you said, my siblings may never understand the depth of my loss, and there's nothing I can do about that. But the special care our dad gave me after her passing showed me how to be a strong, caring man under the worst of circumstances. Dad's gone, too, but I think the Lord was using him to prepare me for the life we have right now. And as far as I'm concerned…it's absolutely perfect—"

"Perfect?" Samantha's forehead creased. "Even with you having to push me around...like a rag doll in a wheelchair—"

"Baby, I'd push you around the whole, wide world with my bare hands if I had to." Sam's hazel eyes deepened with emotion. "Don't you know that?"

"But—" Samantha fought back her tears. "It's the not knowing that's really killing me, Sam. Will I live? Will I get better, or—"

"I know, baby, and it kills me, too. But all the more reason we have to take our eyes off the unknown and embrace every moment the Lord gives us together—"

"But...there's so little I can do to show you how much I love you, Sam—"

"Samantha—" Sam gently lifted his wife's face and wiped her tears with the warmth of his fingertips. The love between them was electric—built on years of shared respect, trust, and a wealth of experiences. "Your voice, your smile, your touch...they are what I live for each day. And knowing that I can help you go through this...well, it fills my heart with such joy. You being here with me, Samantha...that's all I'll ever ask—"

"Oh, Sam—"

"I love you, Samantha Sterling...just the way you are. You're the only girl for me...then and now...don't you know?" Sam branded a hot kiss on her forehead and gathered her fragile body into his arms.

"Yes, I do," Samantha whispered. It took all of the strength in her weak body to return his warm embrace; but return it, she did. "And I love you, too, Sam Sterling. There is no one else in this whole, wide world I'd rather be married to...in my condition...in any condition...other than you. You've made my life so special and so very complete. You're not only my husband, but you're my best friend—"

"Remember?" Sam smiled with fond recollection. "Remember when we'd walk from campus down to the Chesapeake Bay with our homemade sandwiches in a brown paper bag—"

"Yeah, because we didn't have an extra dime between us." Samantha giggled. "And the water would be the most brilliant shade of blue—"

"Just like our pool is now—"

"And we'd talk for hours about our plans and our future—"

"And how much we loved each other—"

"And how we never wanted to be apart…not ever again—"

"The Lord granted us the desires of our hearts; didn't He?"

"Yes, He did—"

"And for that reason, Samantha, we have nothing to regret and no reason to fear—"

"You've got that right, Sam Sterling!" Samantha perked up like in the old days. "And it's so wonderful to be able to relive precious moments with the man I love."

"Now, that's music to my ears." Sam's broad smile blanketed his weary face. "So, let's catch up like we used to in the old days…with the whole truth and nothing but the truth. What's been on your mind, pretty lady?"

"Well, okay," Samantha said. "I must admit I've been feeling a little…anxious lately—"

"Oh?"

"Well…it's because I haven't had the energy of late to tackle some of the new plans that I'd been working on for our church's food pantry—"

"But Pastor Jamie said everything is running smoothly—"

"I know. I've talked to him this week. He told me the same thing. Fortunately, we're well organized, and we have some great members who consider this as their work of service. But, Sam, you know we were planning an expansion—"

"Expansion?"

"Yes, remember, I told you. We were planning to expand the Soup Kitchen. We'd feed all comers, of course, but we'd also pipe in the Wednesday Bible Study and the Sunday sermon into the kitchen.

In that way, the people being fed the physical food could also be fed the Word of God at the same time—"

"Oh, yes, I recall. So, what's the problem?"

"The problem is me!" Samantha sighed. "I used to have enough energy to pull myself over to that sweet, little sunny corner you set up in my room for my computer. And there I could noodle all of my ideas and sketch them out for the people at the church to complete. But—"

"But?"

"But…since I've been taking these new intravenous drugs that Dr. Wallace prescribed, I'm too tired to make myself concentrate—"

"I understand—"

"No, you don't!" Samantha countered. "I can remember when all this stuff came so easily to me. Even now, I seem to be able to make it through the Zoom calls with the orphanage board okay…because I really don't have to say much. But, sometimes, even when I ask Joy to set my computer on my bed table…my brain…it's like thick pea soup…I just can't concentrate…and, Sam, it really concerns me—"

"I know, baby, but you can't frustrate yourself like that…not now. Pray about it, and let it go. The Lord will make a way…and maybe, it's just not the time for it—"

"I know," Samantha agreed. "You're right…but you know how I am…Miss Johnny-on-the-Spot…but I know…it'll be alright—"

"It will," Sam said. "I'll even talk to Pastor Jamie about it myself if it'll put your mind at ease."

"Yes, would you, please?" Samantha said. "I think you're right. I'd feel better knowing that I'm not dropping the ball or holding up anything. I don't want to be a stumbling block—"

"You've got it!"

"Great! Thanks!"

"And the next time Dr. Wallace stops by, we can mention your concerns to him, as well."

"Good idea." Samantha slowed. "And if I forget to do it, Sam, will you please remember to talk to him about it?"

"Of course, I will—"

"Thanks, Sam, that does put my mind at ease—"

"And…how are things going with you and Nurse Greene?"

"Joy? Oh, she's…just a joy!" Samantha giggled. "She's pleasant and very professional. There's not been a time when she's caused me any pain or discomfort…even with all the needles and the port. The treatment feels warm going in, but that's the only weird sensation. So, I guess to answer your question, Nurse Joy Greene is fine…just fine—"

"You'll let me know if that ever changes—"

"Why would it?"

"No reason." Sam smiled against the gnawing tension in his gut.

"Well, then," Samantha said with a wink and a sly grin, "now that we've solved all of the world's problems…pass me one o' them wicked chocolate chip cookies and my water bottle, please, sir…so I can wash it all down!"

CHAPTER 6

To everyone's delight, Nurse Joy Greene did, in fact, return to the Sterling's residence promptly as planned on Saturday night. Her first week had been a bit rocky, but she was determined not to give up on her aspirations. And like clockwork on Sunday morning, Sam and Mrs. Barnes were sitting on the very back row of the first service at Sandywood Bible Fellowship. Although they routinely wore their masks, they preferred the back row in an attempt to encounter fewer people, and they could make a speedy and inconspicuous exist if there were ever an emergency at home. They received the waves and nods from the familiar faces in the congregation and returned them cheerfully—gratefully. It was good for them to be back in the house of the Lord. When the spirited praise service and warm greetings were completed, the sermon began.

"Good morning, Sandywood!" Pastor Jamie Ridley said enthusiastically as he mounted the pulpit. He was wearing his Christ-is-the-Answer tee shirt, jeans, and sneakers—no socks.

"Good morning, Pastor!" The congregation swelled in reply. Their exuberant faces were filled with glad expectation.

"Well, let's get right down to it," Pastor Jamie said as was his style. "I've got three points for you, and I'll take my seat." He grinned impishly and pushed his scraggly, blonde hair behind his ears. "We do a lot of outreach and service to people through our church, so we need to get some things straight in our minds in order to be effective," he began. "First off…people should have no place in our hearts, our minds, or our souls. Yes, I said what I said…and you heard me right." The pastor smiled broadly. "Our hearts, our minds, and our souls belong to the Lord. And that's where He alone should reside. People should be off limits there. Do you know why?"

the pastor asked rhetorically while staring down at the puzzled faces of his congregation. "Well, I'll tell you why," he said in his blended Southern-East Coast drawl. "People love you for them! Jesus loves you for you!

"Don't believe me? Then, let's think about it." The preacher pressed his hands tightly against the podium. "Try telling somebody something and watch how they immediately start relating it back to themselves. Right? And watch how people see something in you that they either like, want, or need, and they set out to extract it from you. We all do it. We don't mean any harm. But that's the way we roll. That's what we do...even when we don't realize that we're doing it. And, I rush to add, that's why some people get so mad at you when they can't have their way with you...when they can't extract from you the very thing they see and want." Pastor Jamie cocked his head and raised his brows. "Feel me?"

"Yes, Pastor!"

"But Jesus...Jesus is different. Hallelujah! He is not like man. He loves you for you! Everybody else may want something from you, but not Jesus! Jesus came to give something to you...faith, hope, love, salvation, eternal life, and freedom...and His own personal help and protection from day to day. And for that reason, He is the only one we should ever entrust with our whole heart, mind, soul, and strength. These are our *most-precious possessions*. This is our very essence. This is who we are. And the Lord doesn't want anyone else touching, toying with, or breaking you down. Not ever! He's the only one who is able to maintain and sustain our most-precious possessions. Why is He the only one, you may ask? Because! He never dies. He never lies. He has the power to keep every one of His promises. He loves each of us to death, and He's already proven it. And there is no one else in this whole, wide world who loves you like that. No-body!" The pastor boomed.

"Consequently, we are to put no one before Jesus Christ. He alone is Lord. He alone gets to call the shots in our lives. And He makes it plain in Luke 10:17: 'Thou shalt love the Lord thy God with *all* thy heart, and with *all* thy soul, and with *all* thy strength, and with *all* thy mind; and thy neighbor as thyself.' And *all* means *all*! Now, that puts a great big damper on this whole soul-mate notion, huh? Because Jesus is the only one worthy of being our soulmate. And if you ask me, that's why folk get so overly distressed when relationships break-up and people die—" The mike squawked just in time to cut off the pastor's rant, and the congregation giggled nervously.

"But…I digress," the pastor admitted and reclaimed his central theme. "Second of all…that same scripture says, we are to love and serve people…*as ourselves*…not more than ourselves…not better than ourselves…not less than ourselves. We are to love and serve people as an act of worship to our Lord. Our service is simply our way of glorifying Christ, and He is our sole audience. We do what He's called us to do, and we leave all the outcomes in His hands. We can help people on the outside, but only Jesus can help people on the inside. Because only Jesus can change a heart and touch a soul.

"And if you ever think what you do for people will move the needle on how much they love you, you are sadly mistaken. In fact, the more you do for some folk; the more they'll hate you. So, then…we love and serve people, expecting nothing from them in return. In fact, if you stop and think about it, the only time we ever get really disappointed or hurt is when we give people our love and expect them to love us in return. Am I right?"

"Why, yes…that is right!" One grateful heart in the audience swelled.

"Glad we agree!" Pastor Jamie chuckled. "And we don't ever want to hear ourselves say: 'After all I've done for them, and they don't love me no better than this!'" The pastor used his most comical voice, but he also took that moment to make serious eye contact with his rapt audience. He accepted their affirmative nods as a sign of agreement. "No, we don't ever want to get to that day," he reiterated.

"And we don't ever have to get to that day because we're going to learn and start operating in the truth to-day. The truth is…love is not a debt, or a hook, or a prison cell, or a place to hold people captive. Love is not tit-for-tat. Love is not a tool or a bargaining chip that seeks to control or extract from others what we need or want for ourselves. You can't buy it. You can't barter for it. You can't even sell-off your soul for it. True love is totally free!"

Pastor Jamie stepped from behind the pulpit with outstretched arms. "Love is the Spirit of Christ that has been given to each of us who have faith to believe. Jesus was freely given to us; He is to be freely shared by us with others. So, Sandywood, we are to simply love and serve others with a made-up mind that the Lord's way is right and to point them to His cross. For Jesus said it in John 14:6: 'I am *the* way, *the* truth, and *the* life: no man cometh unto the Father, but by me.'"

"Amen!" the attentive congregation chorused in unity.

"Third thing, and I'm out," the pastor said, rushing to his close. "We can render aide, but we cannot save any-body. We can't change who people are. For a person to be saved, they have to accept Jesus Christ for themselves. Salvation is of the Lord. Salvation is an individual calling that has nothing to do with us. Only Jesus died for the sins of the world…not us. Only Jesus was able to bury our sins in the grave and to rise again…not us. Only Jesus saves, delivers, and sets free…not us. We're not able to hold people and things together. In Christ, all things consist…not in us. So, we can't do it for others; we can only accept Jesus Christ for ourselves. We teach, and preach, and live the Gospel, but each individual has the right and freewill to accept it or to reject it; and there is nothing we can do about it."

The pastor fought back tears of compassion. "But…we have the Lord's precious promise in Romans 10:9: 'If *you* shalt confess with *your* mouth the Lord Jesus, and shalt believe in *your* heart that God hath raised Him from the dead, *you* shalt be saved.' And verse 13 says it more plainly: 'For *whosoever* shall call upon the name of the

36

Lord shall be saved.' And that, my brothers and sisters, is the Good News of the Gospel of Jesus Christ!"

Pastor Jamie pushed back his long, blonde locks and regained his glowing smile. "So, Sandywood, keep fasting; keep praying; keep abiding in His love. Read your Bible…it is the Bread of Life…and follow the Lord's lead. For He has promised in His Word to be with us and to take us all the way from here to Glory. And in Him, we can put our whole faith; our whole trust; and rest our lives upon His precious promises…and, then, we'll be able to freely share His love with others wherever we go. You see, Jesus Christ must be the only resident in our hearts…because everything else and everybody else is passing away. Amen?"

"Amen, Pastor!" the congregation resounded as one joyful spirit, including Sam Sterling and Mrs. Barnes. Simple, plain speech—tied directly to the Bible—was what the entire congregation loved about Pastor Jamie; and their love was bearing fruit. In fact, it was after one of his simple sermons like this that Samantha Sterling had been given the idea to start-up the church's free food bank—The Bread of Life Food Pantry.

Pastor Jamie and his wife, Melissa, stood outside the church in hopes of greeting everyone as they passed, but their little, towheaded twin boys were making it a challenging undertaking. Nonetheless, Sam Sterling and Mrs. Barnes made the attempt.

"Hello, Pastor Jamie…Melissa," Sam said. "Mighty fine sermon this morning."

"Well, we're just glad that you and Mrs. Barnes could make it." Pastor Jamie smiled. "How's Mrs. Sterling doing?"

"She's having a good morning, Pastor," Sam said to the beat of Mrs. Barnes' agreeable nods. "And she asked me to give you both her love. She's got a new, full-time nurse now, and they seem to be hitting it off just fine."

"That's certainly good to hear," Pastor Jamie said. "Please give her our love as well as our thanks for taking the time from her bed to continue the church's food pantry—"

"Yes, I need to call you about that very thing," Sam said. "But if you'll excuse us for now, we must say hello to Rufus before he gets away—"

"Of course…be blessed." The pastor and his wife waved farewell while wrestling with their active little boys—one in each hand.

"Hi, Chief," Sam said, flagging the older man down, "how's it going?"

"Oh, hi, Sam…Mrs. Barnes…good to see both o' y'all," Chief Rufus Outlaw said warmly, craving a handshake, but opting instead for appropriate social distancing. He had a hoarse, southern accent that was quite engaging, and he'd recently adopted wearing a 10-gallon police hat that was fast becoming his pride and joy. In fact, if they weren't situated smack-dab in the backwoods of Georgia, he could've easily been mistaken for a tall, dark, and handsome Texas cowboy—boots and all. "Well, you know how it is," the chief said, tipping his hat and slapping one knee, "mine is the only profession where business is best when you ain't got much of it."

Rufus Outlaw was, in fact, the newly-elected police chief, and it was largely due to the backing from Sam, the pastor, and his church family—and he knew that right well. They constituted a lot of votes and wielded a wealth of influence in the community. So, it was no wonder he was often quoted as saying, "Without Sam Sterling's bankroll and my church's sway, how else could a black man like me come skrait-up out the sawmill and become the Chief of Police in a town like Sandywood, Georgia? How else?"

CHAPTER 7

"Welcome home, Sam!" Joy swung open the front door when they returned from the first service. I was telling Mrs. Barnes, here, that I don't get to go to church much in my line of work…and I'm sure you can understand that—"

"Perfectly," Sam said as he and Mrs. Barnes squeezed passed her to enter the foyer. "And, of course, I appreciate your staying here with Samantha so that we could attend—"

"Oh, that was absolutely no problem at all," Joy said, trailing them into the kitchen. "But as you can see, I'm dressed and ready to go." She tossed back her long, flowing curls over a perfectly-fitting navy dress. It was complemented by a classic, double strand of freshwater pearls and earrings to match. "Because as I said to Mrs. Barnes, I think I would really enjoy attending second service. That is…if that's alright with you, Sam—"

"Yes, I see you're dressed and ready," Sam said, "and you look lovely, Joy. I'm sure you'll enjoy Sandywood, and there's absolutely no reason why you shouldn't be able to attend the second service this Sunday…or any Sunday that you choose—"

"Oh, I was hoping to hear you say that, Sam," Joy said. She was flirting so hard; she was sucking up all the oxygen in the room.

"Oh, my Lord—" Mrs. Barnes clucked her tongue and ambled over to the kitchen sink so she could roll her eyes in peace. *That girl may be pretty, and she may be smart, but she ain't got a lick o' sense in her whole head. Mooning over Mr. Sterling like some love-sick puppy…with his sick wife just upstairs in her bedroom. Lord o' mercy!*

"Well, Samantha has had a really good morning." Joy fluttered. "She's had her treatment, and she's napping now. And I'll be right back after the service—"

"Take your time, Joy," Sam said, turning to Mrs. Barnes who was re-washing some invisible dishes in the sink. "We've got this covered. And if we all attend the same church fellowship, we can all stay on one accord in this household. Wouldn't you agree, Mrs. Barnes?"

"Um-hmm. Right. Sure thing, Mr. Sterling." Mrs. Barnes' voice crackled with annoyance, but she was making every attempt at civility. "I'm sure you'll enjoy the second service, Nurse Greene…as much as Mr. Sterling and I enjoyed the first—"

"I'm sure I will, too—"

"'Cause as Pastor was saying, 'We can lend a hand…but only Jesus can fix a heart,'" Mrs. Barnes recited, sweeping her eyes over Joy as though she were examining a prime candidate for a serious heart transplant. "So, I'll just put you on my prayer list—"

"Well…alrighty then…you just do that, Miz Barnes," Joy said while issuing Sam a sly, dismissive twinkle, "and I'll be sure to do the same for you." And without so much as skipping a beat, she swirled on her navy stilettos, retrieved her matching purse, and pranced toward the front door. "Thanks, again, Sam! Toodles!"

****

Joy slipped on her mask when she arrived late for the second service at Sandywood Bible Fellowship. She could've made it on time, but she was definitely in no hurry. Being a tad-bit late gave her the opportunity to make her grand entrance just as Pastor Jamie was taking the podium. Against the kind usher's stern protest, Joy made her way down to the very front row. As she strolled the aisle, she spotted the petite, red-headed lady who must've been the pastor's wife because she was wrestling with a set of rambunctious twin boys. As she took her seat, Joy also noticed that this church wasn't much bigger than her home church back in Kansas City. But unlike her home church, with its stained-glass windows and prominent steeple, this was just a utilitarian, multi-functional space with not much to distinguish it from one of the local big-box stores—with the startling exception of the giant, rugged cross suspended behind the pulpit.

Pastor Jamie preached some of the same truths he had at the first service. However, his climax was somewhat different. He ended his sermon with: "Don't be burdened down with the cares of this world. Every person to their own choices. We don't love and serve to get results. We serve to show Christ's love to the world; and that, my dear brothers and sisters, is our singular mission."

However, the entire message was lost on Joy because she was too busy sizing up her new territory. On her walk down the center aisle, she'd also noticed that the congregation was made up mostly of common folk. Sure, she'd spotted a sprinkling of prominent lawyers, bankers, and other professionals by their distinctive dress; but for the most part, this was a congregation of haves and have-nots, and she had every intention of aligning herself with the haves. *What is Sam Sterling…millionaire businessman…doing hanging-out with this mixed-multitude? He deserves so much better than this. He deserves…me! And when I get my turn at being Mrs. Sam Sterling, I'll make it my mission to get us away from this woeful crowd and align ourselves with the movers-and-shakers in this world.*

After the service, Joy was sure to take off her mask outside so that everyone could have a perfect view of the newcomer in their midst. Of course, she kept an appropriate distance, but she made every effort to introduce herself to Pastor Jamie and his family. And with the same level of church-anity that she'd mastered at Greater Harvest Christian Church of Kansas City, she said, "My-my, Pastor Jamie…that was such a darling sermon…and all of it so very true. And it's so good to finally meet you and your lovely wife…and these two, cute little boys. Lord, love 'em!" She smiled to show off her perfectly white teeth. "I've heard so much about you and your dynamic ministry from Sam…Sam Sterling. I'm his new nurse…Joy Greene."

"Well, we're certainly glad to meet you," the pastor said, turning to his wife. "Sam had mentioned to me and Melissa earlier that Mrs. Sterling is receiving constant care, but he failed to mention what a pretty young lady you are. Isn't she, Melissa—"

"Oh, yes, she certainly is the pretty one," Melissa said while the twins were taking turns doing whirlies off the tail-end of her skirt.

Joy smiled sweetly and presented her best face, but those words brought back a flood of memories. As she politely dismissed herself and ambled over to her gold BMW, she drifted back to the first time she'd heard herself being called *the pretty one*. And as she recalled, it had been at church then, too—at her home church in Kansas City. Although she'd been only six or seven years old, it felt like only yesterday.

Oh, yes…I remember. How could I ever forget? My cousin, Hope, and I were swinging hands and skipping out of church that Sunday after worship service alongside our mothers when Sister Victoria Armstrong showed up. Sister Armstrong thought she was real hot stuff, with her phony-acting self. She was a big name in the church, and she was the Director of the Youth Department. I can almost hear her hoity-toity voice right now—

****

"Well, if it's not the Greene twins…just who I wanted to see," Sister Victoria Armstrong said, as she waddled over to our mothers. "I'm planning a big extravaganza to raise much-needed funds for the Youth Department, and I'd like your daughters, Hope and Joy, to participate. We're having a beauty pageant and talent contest, and I think Hope and Joy will make a big hit modeling together on our program. You know everyone loves your girls. They even call them *the twin cousins*. And won't they look so cute hitting the runway together…hand-in-hand?" She snorted noisily. "Everyone will just love it! It will bring the house down!"

"I'm so very sorry," my mother said when she'd learned of the date of the event, "but Joy will be away at a piano recital on that weekend." Then turning to her twin sister, Faith, she said, "But, maybe, Hope can do it—"

"Oh, no, no…that would never do!" Sister Armstrong shrieked, flapping her arms like a scalded duck. "We all love Hope, of course, we do. She is such a nice little girl…with those big, brown eyes and that sweet, little ole dimple. But, as you know, Joy…well…Joy is *the pretty one*. Everyone says so—"

****

Of course, the poor woman had tried to whisper that last part for our mothers' ears only, but Hope and I overheard her…loud and clear…and neither of us ever forgot it either. And from that day forward, the die was cast in our hearts and in our minds. Of the twin cousins, Hope Greene is 'the nice one", but Joy…Joy Greene is 'the pretty one'. "And, she was absolutely right," Joy crowed to herself as she revved-up her BMW and shot out of the church's parking lot. "I most certainly am! So, look out, Sam Sterling, I'm about to cash-in all of my chips to win your heart. Ha!"

CHAPTER 8

On the next Monday morning, bright and early, Dr. Wallace rang the front doorbell at 2200 Bird of Paradise Road. "Good morning, Mrs. Barnes. I'm here to check on Mrs. Sterling...uh...Samantha."

"Of course, Doc, come right on in." Mrs. Barnes smiled broadly. "I wasn't expecting you...thought you were scheduled to come next week—"

"Yes, that would've been my regularly scheduled time, but since I've prescribed this new treatment for Samantha, I thought I'd better check-in on her today. I cleared it with Sam—"

"Oh, no matter," Mrs. Barnes said, swinging open the front door. "You're always welcome."

"Where're Sam and Nurse Greene?"

"Sam's in his office downstairs. I'll fetch him," Mrs. Barnes offered. "And Nurse Greene...well, the nurse is upstairs with Mrs. Sterling—"

"Is there something wrong?" Dr. Wallace's concern matched the deep creases in his forehead.

"Well, Doc...not really." Mrs. Barnes forced a stiff smile and rechecked her attitude. "It's just that at times...that young lady sets my teeth on edge...rubs me the wrong way—"

"Is that a problem?"

"Naw, Doc. Every dog's got his day—"

"Pardon?

"I'm just saying; let it run its true course." Mrs. Barnes shrugged. "Maybe, it's me. Maybe, I'm getting old and set in my ways...used to ruling the roost, you know...old school vs. new school—"

"Oh, I see." Dr. Wallace's concern turned into a sly wink and a chuckle. "But if it ever becomes a problem, you will let me know—"

"Oh, not to worry, Doc. Ain't been a female born yet that I can't handle." Mrs. Barnes added a wink and took a sassy stroll over to the intercom. "I know you can find your way upstairs, and I'll let Mr. Sterling know you're here."

"Good morning, Samantha," Dr. Wallace greeted behind a slight tap on her bedroom door. "Hello, Nurse Greene, how is our beautiful patient this morning?"

"Good morning, Dr. Wallace," Joy replied, "Samantha is—"

"Let's have none of that!" Samantha coughed out her reply. "Samantha is…present…and Samantha can…speak for herself…at least for now—"

"Oh, I beg your pardon—" Joy bristled.

"Well, it's good to see that both of you ladies are alert and in fine fiddle this morning," the doctor said as he approached Samantha's bedside. "So, how have you been feeling, Samantha?"

"I don't know, Doc—"

"She's been more tired than usual, and she's having problems concentrating," Sam said as he slowly ambled into the room.

"Oh, really?" The doctor turned to Nurse Greene. "I've had no reports of this from your nurse—"

"Well, to be honest," Samantha intervened, "I've only told my husband how I've really been feeling—"

"Yes, Dr. Wallace," Sam said, "that's correct."

"Well, we'll have to see what we can do about it." Dr. Wallace side-eyed Nurse Greene. "Has her port been functioning properly?"

"Yes, doctor," Joy clipped. "There've been no problems and no incidents with the equipment."

"Doc…Joy hasn't caused me any discomfort," Samantha said, speaking up in her defense. "It's me. I'm just really off my game…in the thinking department—"

"And that's a real concern for my wife." Sam firmed.

"So, what're you trying to do that takes such brain power?" Dr. Wallace's eyes narrowed. "Why aren't you focusing on resting and getting better?"

"I oversee the food pantry at my church," Samantha explained. "And we're planning...an expansion...and I need to be able to...to develop...expansion plans...and I'm having the hardest time...and it used to be so easy—"

"Oh, I see." Dr. Wallace turned to Sam. "Well, after examining the blood samples received from Nurse Greene, I've determined that some elements of Samantha's current treatment need to be modified. I've made those adjustments for her new doses going forward...and, maybe, that will do the trick in terms of improving her stamina—"

"You think so, Dr. Wallace?" Samantha said hopefully.

"Yes, I do—"

"And in the meantime," Joy spoke up loudly so all could hear, "it would be my pleasure to assist you with whatever plans you need to develop—"

"Really?" Samantha's smile blossomed. "Joy, you'd do that for me?"

"Sure thing," Joy said, searching Sam's eyes for an approving glance. "Sandywood Bible is my church now, too, and I'd be happy to assist you in any way that I can. You can tell me what you want done on the computer or at the church, and I'll gladly do it for you. It's the least I can do—"

"That's a fine offer, Joy," Sam said. "I could get Pastor Jamie to show you around the church after second service next Sunday, and you could get a feel for Samantha's vision for the food pantry and for the modifications to the Soup Kitchen. Samantha wants the people who're receiving the physical food to have access to the spiritual food, as well, from Bible Study to the Sunday sermon. And, right now, she needs help finding ways to get that done."

"That's an incredible undertaking, Sam!" Joy said eagerly. "And that suits me just fine. I'm looking forward to getting to know Pastor

Jamie and his wife a whole lot better. They seem to be really fine people—"

"Oh, thanks, Joy," Samantha said. "I can't tell you how much that really puts my mind at ease. Two heads are certainly better than one…especially when one feels like it's wading through…thick pea soup—"

"And putting your mind at ease is certainly what we want to do," Dr. Wallace said. "You are, first of all, my patient, Samantha, and I want you resting and getting stronger…not hurrying or worrying about anything."

"Right," Sam said. "The new medications will get you stronger, and Joy's assistance will set your mind at ease. And I'm sure the combination will do wonders for you, baby—"

"You're right, my love," Samantha said, gently squeezing her husband's strong hand. "Sounds like the perfect plan. Thanks, guys. We sure do make a great team!"

CHAPTER 9

"Well, hello there, Nurse Greene—"

"It's Joy—"

"Alrighty then…it's Joy!" Pastor Jamie offered her a broad smile followed by an animated fist bump. "My wife, Melissa, wanted to join us today on this after-service church tour, but our boys need their nap—"

"Oh, I really do understand," Joy said, returning his smile with a brilliant one of her own. "And I hate to pull you away from all of your *daddy-duties*…because I'm sure your wife needs all the help she can get with your twin boys—"

"No worries." Pastor Jamie's smile stiffened at her insinuation that his sons were an incorrigible duo. "My wife is perfectly capable of handling our sons on her own. And just so you know, they're not the frightful handful at home that they appear to be in public." He added a nervy chuckle. "Sometimes, I think being around our lively congregation gives my little boys the *silly-willies*—"

"If you say so—"

"So, what would you like to see first, Joy? I guess we should start with our Soup Kitchen so you can see the place in full swing. It serves around 100 folks on any given Wednesday and sometimes double that number each Sunday." Pastor Jamie took the lead, guiding them on their tour. "Right this way."

"Wow, this is truly amazing!" Joy gasped. "I really expected to see only men, you know…winos, derelicts, bums…but look at this! They're women…children…and even families…all getting fed right here…together."

"Indeed." Pastor Jamie nodded approvingly. "The fields are ripe for harvest. That's why Mrs. Sterling wants to share God's word with all the people who enter our church doors, whether they come through the front door or the kitchen door. We want to touch each soul. We never know who the Lord might call to be saved.'

"And the quality of the food is not at all what I expected," Joy admitted. "I had in mind a big, steaming pot of soup and a crust of bread—"

"Oh, no, not at all!" Pastor Jamie grinned. "And that's because some of the finest restaurants in the county have agreed to donate food every Wednesday and every Sunday. And these are not leftover scraps. These are healthy meals, planned especially for our guests, because that's the agreement Mrs. Sterling made with all of the food establishments; and they've pretty much stayed true to course. And our congregation is well-known for supporting the businesses who support us. You'd be surprised what people will do to help others if you just ask them with the right spirit."

"Really?"

"And Mrs. Sterling is the champion of diplomacy. People see her good heart from a mile away, and they respond to her efforts in kind. I'm sure by now you've noticed that God-given quality about her—"

"Sure—" Joy clicked her tongue, refusing to give the idea a moment's thought. "So, what is it she wants to do here… Samantha, I mean?"

"We've got to figure out a way…an economical way…to get the place wired for sound so the Bible studies and the sermons can be heard by the folks who're here in the kitchen—"

"That should be no problem," Joy said. "I'm sure they're plenty of companies around here, or in the Atlanta area, that would jump at the chance to get a contract of this size—"

"Sure. But our budget for this project is limited," Pastor Jamie explained. "We've got so many programs going on at this church; no one of them can eat up a lion's share of the budget."

"Point taken." Joy agreed. "Well, what about this?" she said. "What if I were to reach out to some of the companies in the area and try to get them to do it for a lower fee…us being a non-profit and a church, and all. Maybe, a few of them would even agree to work together so it would be less burdensome on any one of them. You know…as a team…to build-up goodwill for their companies in the community. Whatcha think?"

"Well, it's sure worth a try," Pastor Jamie said. "Mrs. Sterling has already scribbled out some rough schematics for the project. We could run those by the companies; let them know that we're a humble church trying to bless the less fortunate; and see if they're willing to partner with us—"

"Sounds like a great plan," Joy said, "And I can get started right away—"

"Are you sure you can take this on with all of your nursing duties—"

"Of course, I can!" Joy swelled. "Anything to help Sam and the church. Plus, it'll put Samantha's mind at ease, and that'll be one less thing that Sam has to worry about—"

"Is that so?" The pastor's brows raised. "Well, I can see you're fired up about this, but be sure to run your ideas pass Mrs. Sterling first—"

"Sure thing, Pastor." Joy's eyes widened convincingly. "If I'm nothing else, I'm a true team player—"

"Well, alright," Pastor Jamie said, seemingly unconvinced. There was something about her vibe that troubled him, but he couldn't put his finger on it. "I'm glad to hear you say that, and I'm glad to have your word on it."

"Of course!" Joy shrilled. "Thank you, Pastor. I really appreciate your vote of confidence—"

"Oh, hey, Chief!" Pastor Jamie said, adding a hearty handshake. "Didn't know this was the day for your work of service in the kitchen?"

"It sure is," Chief Outlaw said. "In fact, my shift is nearly over, and it's a good thing. I've gotta get back to the station."

51

"Well, Chief, I'd like to introduce you to someone," the pastor said. "This pretty lady is Joy Greene; and, Joy, this is our brand-new Chief of Police, Rufus Outlaw."

"Is that so?" Joy glimmered. "Well, it's great to meet you, Chief, and I'm sure congratulations are in order."

"Why, thank you, Miz Greene." Chief Outlaw tipped his hat with a smile. "In fact, I think I spied you the other Sunday when you were here—"

"Yes, I was here last Sunday. How kind of you to notice." Joy giggled, happy that her plan to be seen by the locals was working famously. "But, actually, Chief Outlaw, I have a title, too." Joy tossed back her dark curls and supplied him with a riveting smile. "I'm actually *Nurse* Joy Greene. I'm Sam Sterling's new nurse…for his wife, I mean…Samantha. I assume you know Sam."

"Why, indeedy, I do," Chief Outlaw said. "I'm well-acquainted with Mr. Sterling…and Mrs. Sterling, too. I'm sure they're glad to have your expert services, Nurse Greene." And then his left eyebrow twitched. It almost always twitched when he was conflicted between making nice with his face and sniffing out trouble with his nose.

"Oh, snap!" Joy said as she fumbled around in her purse. "Sorry, Pastor, it's my phone. I'll have to catch this; never know when Sam might need me—"

"Of course, you grab your phone call, and I'll whirl you around the rest of our facility on another day when my wife can join us. How about that?"

"Sounds like a plan—"

"Goodbye, Nurse Greene…uhh, Joy—" Pastor Jamie waved, and he and Chief Outlaw moved away out of earshot.

"Oh, so, it's Sam and Samantha, is it?" Chief Outlaw drawled in a gruff whisper. "You mean to tell me she's been around here for less than a hot minute, and she's already calling her new employers by their first names…and referring to her patient like she's less than an afterthought? Pastor Jamie, is this new nurse for real?"

"Well, Sam says she comes highly recommended, and she's very competent." The pastor raised his brows, and the two men got an eye-full as Joy twisted away toward her gold-toned BMW in her red, short skirt and stilettos.

"Hello…this is Nurse Greene—"

"Oh, is it now?"

"Who's this?"

"Joy…you don't recognize the voice of your one and only cousin—"

"What? My cousin? My one and only *twin* cousin?" Joy shouted. "Hope! Gurrl!"

"Sorry to startle you, but I'm on my new business phone—"

"No problem. How are you?"

"Good…but been better—"

"Oh, no! Your mom and dad alright?"

"Calm down! It's nothing like that." Hope soothed. "Mom and Dad are fine, and they send you their love—"

"Okay…you scared me—"

"But there is a death in the family—"

"Who?"

"Uncle Jude—"

"Uncle Jude?"

"Yup…afraid so," Hope clipped. "Mom and Dad got the bad news last week; and, Joy, they're insisting that I go to the funeral in Atlanta—"

"Why you? Why can't they go?"

"They just can't. Their health won't allow it."

"So, are they doing poorly?"

"You know; no worse than usual," Hope explained. "But Daddy is on a breathing machine, and Mom's got crippling arthritis that prevents her from traveling. They're just not up to it, but they say our family needs to represent…even though they haven't seen hide nor hair of the man in over 20 years."

"Yeah, he did leave Kansas City kinda abruptly when we were pretty young…and he never came back—"

"Good riddance!" Hope barked. "I never cared much for the man—"

"Yeah, he could be kinda creepy…always rocking me on his knee and whispering, 'Joy, you sure are the pretty one—'"

"So, Joy…can you come to the funeral with me?" Hope's jaws crackled with annoyance. "Afterall, you do live in Atlanta—"

"When is it?

"Next Wednesday at the funeral home. I guess the funeral home scheduled it mid-week because they really weren't expecting anyone to come—"

"Wednesday? That's out of the question, Hope—"

"But why?"

"I'm a nurse with a brand-new hospice patient…nearly 100 miles away…and I'm only off duty on Fridays and Saturdays—"

"But Joy, I need your moral support—"

"And you've got it…always…but just not in the A-T-L on next Wednesday—"

"Joy, I really don't want to go either—"

"I hear you. I know it's your parents' idea, but I just can't swing it. I've got too much on my plate already. Besides, I've got some pretty hot plans of my own in the works—"

"Oh, okay." Hope sighed. "I understand."

"But it's a shame this all has to fall on you—"

"I know—"

"But since you'll be in the area, why don't you drive down and visit me after the funeral?"

"Could I do that?"

"Sure, you can." Joy's voice smiled. "You could drive down for lunch and be back at the airport before your return flight to K.C. I can get Mrs. Barnes to lay out a fabulous meal for us. Whatcha say?"

"Who's Mrs. Barnes?"

"Oh, she's just the live-in help, but she's a great cook…and I'm sure she'd love to meet you. She's always pestering me about my family tree—"

"Well, this trip would make a whole lot more sense if I were coming to visit the living rather than burying the dead—"

"Well, that much we agree on. So, if you can swing it, let me know. Okay? I'll make all the necessary arrangements on this end."

"That's sweet of you, Joy." Hope giggled. "It's always good talking to my *twin cousin*. We've really got to do this more often—"

"You've got that right," Joy said. "So, don't you dare disappoint me. I expect to see you, just let me know when."

"Will do. Love you, Joy—"

"Of course, you do. What's not to love? Bye!"

CHAPTER 10

"Joy-y…I'm lost!"

"Lost?!? Hope, where are you?"

"I thought I put your address into the rental car's GPS correctly, but it took me to Sandybrook not Sandywood! Where am I?"

"I don't know. Let me ask Mrs. Barnes—"

"Yes…please—"

"Well, Mrs. Barnes says you've gone about 75 miles out of the way. Sandybrook is due east of us."

"Oh, if I have to backtrack 75 miles, I'll never get there in time for lunch—"

"Oh, never mind that. Just log us back into your vehicle's GPS *and* on your phone…and, Hope, pay attention this time—"

"But I thought I did last time—"

"Never mind! You're always getting lost. Just be careful and get here when you can."

"I will. I'll stop for gas and be on my way," Hope said. "I'll text you when I get close."

"Yes, please do…because I'm looking forward to seeing my one-and-only twin cousin…real soon!"

Hope pulled into the nearest gas station to freshen up and get her bearings. *Well, I guess it is my fault. I should've been paying closer attention to my driving…but how can I when that funeral has me so rattled? All I can think about is the last time I saw Uncle Jude alive. I've tried to forget it…oh, how I've tried! But every time I think I'm breaking free…that horrible memory creeps back in to haunt me. It's like a dark cloud hanging over my life!*

****

"Of course, I'll always remember the night of the big family party. I remember it like it was yesterday!" Hope mumbled to herself as she sped along the highway. Try as she might, she couldn't resist rehearsing it aloud once again—the terrible turn of events that she'd been so desperately trying to forget.

"Yes, it was the night of our family's double celebration. On the Sunday, shortly after our eighth birthday, I was sitting on the front pew at church beside my cousin, Joy. All of a sudden, I was grabbed by the Gospel message, and I couldn't resist its pull. The love of Jesus Christ and the salvation that He promised seemed to lift me right off my seat. And when it was time to go forward for the altar call, I gave Joy my hand; and like always, she took it. And then, there we were, me and Joy, side-by-side at the altar, confessing our faith in Jesus Christ, and the pastor was giving us the right hand of fellowship. Pastor Jones, our parents, and the whole congregation were so very excited. And to everyone's delight, Joy and I were baptized the following Sunday—together.

"But as it turned out, on that very same Sunday, the Deacon Board had announced its slate of new deacons. The newly-elected deacons included Joy's daddy and mine...the Greene twins...and two other men. However, our daddy's older brother, Uncle Jude, had not been chosen.

"So, on the next Sunday evening, we all had that big family party. Joy and I were celebrating our baptism, and both of our daddies were celebrating their induction into the Deacon Board. Uncle Jude came to the party, but it was plain to see he was none too happy. He would never admit it, of course, but everyone knew he wanted to be a deacon. He thought by him being the eldest son of their revered, deceased daddy, Deacon Isaiah Greene, he was owed a slot on the Deacon Board. He believed it was his birthright. But evidently, the deacons didn't agree because they'd given the prestigious honor to his younger, twin brothers instead—James and John.

"We all knew that Uncle Jude was hot under the collar; but in spite of it, everyone was pretending to have a great time. I saw Uncle Jude rocking Joy on his knee and whispering in her ear as he often did. I even overheard him saying, 'Joy, you know you're the pretty one!' He did that quite often when our parents weren't around; and every time he did it, he'd sneer at me to let me know he was purposely excluding me. But even at that tender age, I knew he was trying to drive a wedge between me and Joy, and I wasn't having it. So, I simply ignored him and pretended not to care. And since I never really liked him anyway, I just tried to stay out of Uncle Jude's way as much as possible.

'Don't be bitter, Jude,' I heard my dad say that night at the party, trying to clear the air with his big brother. 'Of course, we're all sorry the Deacon Board didn't select you this time around—'

'No worries!' Uncle Jude clapped back as was his way. 'I don't need your pity! I'm just the big brother who's been kicked to the curb ever since you twins were born. I'm used to it—'

'No, Jude, that's not it at all,' Joy's dad said, taking up the plea. 'But maybe…if you were married…you know, a family man and all. Maybe, the Deacon Board would look on you more favorably—'

'Sure thing!' my dad agreed quickly. 'If you were married, Jude, you'd be a shoe-in—'

'Stop it!' Uncle Jude's eyes blazed. 'Of course, I admire you and your *lovely* wives…your neat, little *boring* families, but that's not the life for me. I've never met…a woman…that does it for me—'

'At least, not yet—' My mother inserted with a giggle, trying to cool down the hot temperatures in the room.

'Sure…not yet.' Uncle Jude's nostrils flared as he reluctantly conceded the point.

'It's just a matter of time, Jude,' my dad reassured him. 'Now that John and I are on the Deacon Board, we'll make sure you get in when the time is right—'

'Don't bother!' Uncle Jude's temper sparked again. 'I don't need your stinking handouts. Besides, I've been thinking about blowing this one-horse town anyway and going someplace where my skills and abilities will be greatly appreciated...someplace that offers more opportunities for a Renaissance man such as myself—'

'Ooo-wee! Ouch-ee!' I cried, clutching my upset tummy.

'What's the matter, Hope, too much excitement?' My mom said as she rushed to my aide.

'No-no—' I was forced to confess. 'Too much icing—'

'Icing? But you've only had one piece of cake and ice cream like the rest of us—'

'Not really, Mommy...I...I snuck two cupcakes out of the fridge before the party.' By this time, I'm sure my face was turning an ugly shade of purple because I felt like I needed to upchuck. 'Oww-ee!'

'Well, it serves you right, young lady,' my mom said, quickly marching me upstairs to the bathroom. 'Just for that, you're going to bed early," she said. 'Come, Joy, it's getting late. I'll tuck both of you into bed.'

'No, Auntie Faith! Please, no! Joy had whined. 'I want to stay down here at the party. Besides, I didn't do anything bad—'

'Well, alright, Joy.' Both of our mothers agreed. 'You can stay with us for another hour, but then you've got to go upstairs and get some rest. You both have school tomorrow.'

"As I stomped upstairs to the bathroom with my mom, I couldn't see Joy's face, but I knew she was happy it was me and not her who'd gotten into trouble. It was like Joy to want to be the center of attention while I got shuffled off to bed.

'Now, Hope, you know better,' my mom scolded while washing my face with a cool towel. 'You already know too much sugar is bad for your tummy!' Afterwards, she tucked me into bed and covered me with my favorite, fuzzy blanket, and I felt so warm and cozy. Then she left me to go back downstairs and join the party. If I tried, I could hear everyone's voices humming in the distance.

'I want to play my new recital piece for you.' I heard Joy say. 'This one is my favorite from Beethoven, but Hope doesn't know how to play it yet.'

"It was true. Joy was always a better pianist than me. Although we had the same teacher, Joy enjoyed the grueling work of constant practices; I hated it. Joy basked in the limelight of recitals; they wrecked my nerves. I never quite got the knack of putting on a fake face in public.

"So, I was lying there, enjoying the melody, when I heard my bedroom door quietly open and close. I thought it was just my mom coming back to check on me. But suddenly, someone was pressing their hot lips…hard against my mouth. I was so scared. I opened my eyes. I saw…I saw…Uncle Jude. Oh, no! It was Uncle Jude…my Uncle Jude! I couldn't believe my eyes. He pinned me down under his weight. He pressed his hand down hard over my mouth. He growled at me in a mean whisper, 'I'm gonna do to you what all men wanna do to ugly little girls like you. I'd never do this to Joy 'cause she's the pretty one.'

"I couldn't move. I couldn't speak. I couldn't scream. I felt totally helpless. I felt incredibly small. And for the first time in my life, I felt oh, so ugly. While he pressed his knee against my chest, Uncle Jude ripped off his jacket and threw it on my chair. He unbuckled his pants and pushed himself down hard on top of me, stifling my attempted sobs.

"But just in the nick of time, there was a tap at my door. And then it was followed by a much louder knock. 'Sh-hh,' Uncle Jude said in response to the knock as he leapt up from my bed. 'Quiet, please,' he whispered toward the door while squeezing my mouth shut. 'I finally got Hope back to sleep. Keep it down. You'll wake her—'

'But Jude,' my daddy's voice swelled as he shook the doorknob, 'this door is locked!'

'Oh, is it?' Uncle Jude said, fumbling to re-buckle his belt. 'My bad...force o' habit.' And as he approached the door, Uncle Jude turned to me in a nasty growl meant for my ears only. 'If you ever breathe a word of this to anyone,' he buzzed, 'I'll come back and kill you in your beds...all o' you!'

'Jude!' my daddy yelled behind a fierce knock. 'Open this door!'

'Shhh!' Jude hissed, opening the door. 'You're gonna wake up Hope!'

"When the door opened, I squeezed my eyes shut and pretended to be asleep. What else could I do? I was scared out of my mind!

'What's going on in here?' My dad insisted.

'Nothing,' Jude whined. 'I was just passing by Hope's door on my way to the bathroom there, and I heard the poor thing sobbing. She was so unhappy and wide awake. So, I closed the door to block out the music...I guess that's when I locked it by mistake...and, then, I rocked her back to sleep—'

'Well...it appears she's asleep, now.' My dad's voice tightened like a knot on the end of a stiff rope. 'So...I'd say it's time for you to grab-up your jacket over there...off her chair...and let's go—'

'Oh, yeah, my jacket," Uncle Jude fished for words. "Uhh, well, you see, I took it off...didn't want the zipper to scratch baby girl's pretty face—'

'Uh-huh.' My dad's voice was pocked with annoyance. He said, 'John and Grace are leaving now, and Joy is staying overnight with us...and it's time to get her into bed—'

'Well, I guess the party's over,' Jude said. 'So, I'll be running along—'

'Yeah, you do that,' my dad said in a voice rife with anger. 'In fact, let me show you out!'"

****

"Oh, my Lord! I've been over this, and over this, more than a thousand times in my head! Why can't I shake it?!?" Hope shrilled. When she finally realized she was shivering behind the steering wheel, she took in a deep, cleansing breath to steady her nerves. She blinked back the hot tears foaming in her eyes and did her best to focus on the highway. Fortunately, the traffic was light.

I didn't tell anyone what Uncle Jude did to me back then. I didn't even tell Joy. Afterall, she's my twin cousin, and I thought it was my duty to protect her...shelter her from the ugly truth. But...after that night, my life took a drastic turn. Joy was still free to pursue her dreams...her possibilities were endless. But I was saddled with our frightening family secret. It was my burden to bear...mine alone...or at least, so I thought. But what I didn't know...and what I wish I had known so long ago...my daddy finally confided in me just last week when he was trying to convince me to attend Uncle Jude's funeral.

****

"Jude was always an odd duck," my dad said, as he prodded me to attend his funeral. "But he was our brother; and his business was his business; and me and John never wanted to pry. We knew he had some shaky-jake ways, but we always made allowances for him. He already had ought against us...*the twin brothers*...'cause he felt our parents loved us better than him. It wasn't true, of course, but you can't argue with what a man believes in his own heart, whether it be true or false. Hold on—" Daddy stopped abruptly and waved off my concerns as he fell into a violent coughing fit.

"But, now, when I think back on it," he cleared his throat and continued, "we, me and John, we should've nipped Jude's nonsense in the bud back then. He was a sneaky, arrogant, angry man; and we should've kept him and his hateful ways far away from you and Joy.

We could feel the negative influence he was having on you girls, but we didn't know how to deal with it. We were trying so hard to go along to get along; let things slide, you know. He was family; we loved him. Besides, he was in the church…and we all lived in the hope that he'd turn his life around…someday," my daddy said, drooping as though he were finally unstrapping the weight of the world from off his shoulders.

"Even with all his good looks, we never knew Jude to have no lady-friends. You understand? So, we really didn't know who…or what…he was. We were just hoping he wasn't—" Daddy's nostrils flared, and he shook his head as though to perish the thought. "But that night we found Jude in your bedroom…in there with the door locked…none of us quite knew what to think. After that, we had you checked out by a doctor…remember?"

"I do—"

"Well, we lied and said it was for your first annual checkup," Dad admitted. "And we were all very grateful that you appeared to be alright. Ain't no telling what I would've done to the man if he'd ever hurt you or Joy in any way. So, after that night, me and John weren't about to take any more chances with Jude around our two, baby girls…brother or no brother. We didn't know then, and we don't know now, what kind of man Jude truly was, but we knew we had to get him far away from here. We wanted to keep you and Joy safe from him…like we would from any other over-grown man—"

"But Daddy—"

"Don't stop me, now, daughter. All of this is so very hard to say—" My daddy waved me off again as he struggled to take each breath. "Well, Jude had already said he wanted to move to Atlanta; and after that night, we encouraged him to do so…quick, fast, and in a hurry. He didn't fight us on the idea. In fact, me and John put up some o' the cash to send him on his way. But, Hope—" My dad's weary eyes pleaded for my understanding. "No matter what…Jude was our big brother; and when a Greene dies, our family must represent. So, I need you to go to Jude's funeral. I need you to do it for me…for us…for the family. Do you hear me, Baby-girl?"

****

"Yes, Daddy! I heard you! I heard you loud and clear!" Hope squared her shoulders in the driver's seat and sniffed back her woeful tears. *But, oh, how I wish you'd told me…entrusted me with the truth…way back then! I thought nobody knew but me! I thought I was all alone! I thought I was going out of my mind! But if I'd known that you grownups knew about Uncle Jude and his hellish ways, maybe, I wouldn't have tried to shoulder the burden of his dirty, little secret all alone! Maybe, if I'd known, my life would've turned out differently. Maybe, I would've been free…free to follow my dreams…just like Joy!*

"Oh, Lord…I feel so betrayed!" Hope hammered the steering wheel with a shaky fist. "All this time! All these wasted years! Oh, my, how it hurts…it hurts so bad!"

Hope looked up just in time to see her exit. "Oops! Getting close to Sandywood. Time to pull myself together. Time to text Joy. Time to let her know. I'm almost there."

CHAPTER 11

"Mrs. Barnes, I just heard from my cousin!" Joy swirled into the kitchen to deliver the good news. "And it seems like Hope is almost here...but it's so late...and we've ruined your wonderful lunch—"

"Don't worry 'bout that none," Mrs. Barnes said kindly. "'Cause the only thing that matters is yo' cousin getting here safely—"

"But—"

"You just go about your duties with Mrs. Sterling, Nurse Greene, and I'll handle everything down here. I'll put my special salads back in the fridge, and I'll fry us up some fresh, hot chicken for dinner—"

"Dinner?"

"Yes, ma'am! Your cousin's gotta join us for dinner now—"

"But—"

"No buts about it," Mrs. Barnes said, "it'll be pitch black 'round here in the next few hours, and your cousin ain't got no business bouncing 'round on these back roads after dark. They can get pretty treacherous—"

"But...her flight—"

"Then she'll just have to change her flight 'cause there ain't no doubt about it. Hope's gotta spend the night with us. I'll see to fixing up one of the guestrooms for her down here on the first floor—"

"But I don't want to put you to all that trouble—"

"Ain't no trouble whatsoever...just good, common sense." Mrs. Barnes braced herself for the tasks at hand. "So, go! Scoot! Get outta my kitchen! Everything'll be fine...just fine."

"Well, this is so very nice of you," Joy said, somewhat softening her stance on Mrs. Barnes' previous behavior toward her. "So, I'll head back upstairs to see about Samantha. Please let me know when Hope arrives."

"Of course, I will…Joy." Mrs. Barnes offered her a kind nod and a tenderhearted smile. *Chile, you just don't know. I'm so happy to see you interested in yo' own-self family for a change…instead o' running-up behind Mr. Sterling like somebody what ain't got good sense…whew!*

Later, when Mrs. Barnes answered the bell, she stood back and took a good look at the newcomer. Finally, she said, "Well, come on in here. You must be Hope…Nurse Greene's cousin. And I've heard so many good things about you."

"Why, thank you, ma'am," Hope said politely. "And you must be Mrs. Barnes. Joy told me you were expecting me."

"Yeah, we were expecting you…about two hours ago. But no nevermind! You're here now…safe and sound…and I'm happy to see ya."

"Yes, ma'am." Hope put on her face mask and entered the front foyer. "I'm so sorry to be late," she explained. "I guess Joy told you…I got lost."

"Yes, she did." Mrs. Barnes snickered. "And that's real easy to do down in these parts. All these old back roads look pretty much the same, especially if you don't know where you're going."

"But I've ruined our lunch." Hope pouted. "And I certainly hope I didn't put you to too much trouble—"

"No trouble at all." Mrs. Barnes smoothed her apron as she led their guest back to the kitchen. "'Cause you likely to see some o' that same stuff for dinner—"

"Dinner?" Hope gaped. "No, ma'am. I've got a flight out tonight at 10 p.m."

"That might be what you planned, Miss Hope, but that ain't what you're gonna do." Mrs. Barnes washed her hands and continued her dinner preparations. "It'll be too dark around here in a few hours for you to go fumbling around. You might as well get ready to spend the night right here with us—"

"But Joy only invited me for lunch—"

"Surely, you can work all that out with Joy and the airlines. You new-fangled girls can do just about anything on a computer." Mrs. Barnes moved adroitly about her kitchen. "So, you and Joy can have a good visit while I get dinner on the table. Then, you can get yo'self some good rest tonight, and I'll fix us a hearty brunch in the morning before you head back to the airport. How's that sound?"

"Well, if you don't think it'll be too much trouble—"

"No, ma'am. It would be more trouble if I had to worry about you sliding your car into one o' these vine-covered ditches. These soft shoulders down here don't play; and at night, you can barely see the center line. So, let's get your Covid test done and out the way so we can all rest easy while you're here." Mrs. Barnes moved over to the intercom. "Nurse Greene, your expected guest has arrived."

Sam Sterling was surprised to see a guest at his dining room table when he emerged from his office at 6 p.m., but he didn't let on. "Good evening," he said politely, "I'm Sam Sterling…Samantha's husband."

"And I'm Hope…Hope Greene," she said, following his cue. "I'm Joy's cousin from Kansas City."

"Well, it's good to meet a member of Nurse Greene's family," Sam said with a happy chuckle and a crisp nod. "So glad you could join us—"

"Oh, Sam," Joy chimed in. "Hope was only supposed to be here for lunch…so we wouldn't disturb you…but she got lost coming down here from Atlanta. She had to go to our Uncle Jude's funeral, you know—"

"No, I didn't know; and I'm very sorry for your loss," Sam said, granting each of them a sober smile. "But it's very good to have both *Hope* and *Joy* in our midst."

"Oh, thank you, sir," Hope said sweetly. "I really appreciate your hospitality, and Mrs. Barnes' delicious home cooking."

"Just make yourself at home." Sam added as his final comment. He was determined to stay out of the conversation and allow the ladies to talk freely.

As the dinner progressed, Joy kept the conversation lively with a variety of childhood stories. "Hope," she said, "do you remember the time we had that big family party to celebrate our baptism?"

"You were baptized...together?" Mrs. Barnes raised a hopeful brow.

"Yes, ma'am," Hope said. "We did everything together when we were kids—"

"And do you remember how blazing hot Uncle Jude got when he found out that our daddies had been hand-picked to be deacons...and he'd been passed over? Ha! I thought his head would explode!" Joy giggled wickedly.

"Joy!" Hope said, giving her a stern eye not to air their family's dirty laundry in front of mere strangers. "I'm sure we can spare Mr. Sterling and Mrs. Barnes all the gory details—"

"Yes, that was one doozy of a party; and if I remember correctly, Hope, you were naughty and had to go to bed early—"

"Joy!" Hope's lips tightened into a straight line, and her eyes clouded over with pain. "Not now, okay—"

"Our dads were so happy that night," Joy continued, ignoring Hope's obvious discomfort. "Sam, did you know that my dad and Hope's dad are twin brothers?"

"No, I don't think you ever mentioned that," Mrs. Barnes said, steering the discussion clear of Sam.

"Our mothers are twin sisters, too."

"Are you saying to me that twin brothers married twin sisters?" Mrs. Barnes chuckled gleefully. "Well, bless yo' heart—"

"That's right," Joy said proudly. "And me and Hope were born on the same day, in the same hospital, on the same floor…just 30 minutes apart—"

"Do tell!" Mrs. Barnes gaped.

"Yup, that's true," Joy said. "Hope's just thirty minutes older than me. And that's why we're not only cousins, but everybody back home calls us, *The Twin Cousins*—"

"Well, my word." Mrs. Barnes clasped her hands together. "That's some story. I guess that's why the two of you are so close."

"Indeed!" Joy said, showing off for Sam's benefit. "Hope and I were really close back then, and we shared just about everything. We both loved science. Hope was going to be the doctor, and I'd be her trusty nurse—" Joy thumbed a finger in Hope's direction. "But this one chickened out—"

"Joy!" Hope's voice agonized, as though she were dealing with a petulant child. "This is certainly not the time and place…and there is way more to the story than you know—"

"Not much more." Joy giggled impishly. "Because I became that great nurse we both dreamed about…dah-dah…but you…you turned tail and ran back home—"

"Okay-alright, Joy…have it your way," Hope said to cap-off the discussion, but the profound sadness that overshadowed her mellow eyes was not lost on Sam. Her kind and gentle way of dealing with Joy's obvious misconceptions had captured his attention.

"So, you were both in the same classes in grade school?" Mrs. Barnes piped in to lighten the mood. "I'll bet that was something for your teachers to behold?"

"Yes, it was," Joy said. "And they always called Hope, *the smart one*—"

"Joy was just as smart," Hope remarked. "But they always called her, *the pretty one*."

They all shared a laugh. And as the dinner progressed, the ladies continued to engage in light pleasantries while Sam drifted off into his own thoughts. *"Twin Cousins?" Hmm. Interesting. But the only family resemblance I see is in their mannerisms...in the tone of their voices. That's it. Fact of the matter, I've never really paid much attention to Joy until now. She's my wife's nurse. Period. But now that I see them together, Joy's sharp edges are starting to show. And they say she's 'the pretty one'? I'd beg to differ! Sure, Joy's got flash...perfect smile; quick wit; golden complexion. But Hope's got that beautiful brown skin with those big, luscious eyes to match. They're like windows to a lovely soul...pools of endless adventure, just begging to be explored. Sure, Joy's shapely in a swimsuit...how could I miss her sunning by the pool? But Hope is shorter, sweeter, thicker...in all the right places. And that gorgeous dimple in her left cheek lights up the whole room every time she smiles. Joy's got a high-maintenance vibe. But Hope is real people. You could share a picnic basket with her in an open field, and she'd have you taking your shoes off to sit a spell. Well, Joy, you may think you're all that, but I see Hope. She's loyal to her family...quiet...sensitive...true. So, in my book, Hope Greene, you are most definitely 'the pretty one'!*

As the voices at the table began to ebb, Sam laid his fork and his wandering thoughts aside. *Whoa! What am I thinking? Thank God, Hope will only be here for just one night!* And at the appropriate moment, he pushed back his chair and said, "Ladies, I've really enjoyed your company, but I must go upstairs and check on my beautiful bride. Very nice to have met you, Hope, and I'd like for you to enjoy our every comfort while you're here."

"Thank you, Mr. Sterling—"

"Sam—"

"Thank you...Sam...for making me feel so welcomed on such short notice. It was good to meet you...and the very best to your wife. I'm sure Joy and I will have a great visit—"

"We sure will, Sam. And it was very good of you—" Joy chimed in quickly, but Sam was already halfway upstairs.

After Mrs. Barnes cleared the dishes, Hope and Joy sat alone at the dining room table and sipped a little homemade peach brandy from Mrs. Barnes' secret stash. "I'm really glad to be here with you, Joy," Hope said, breaking the silence between them.

"And I'm really glad you finally showed up...although, you were late as usual," Joy needled, lowering her voice to a whisper. "And what do you think about Sam?"

"Mr. Sterling? What do you mean?" Hope puzzled. "He's a very nice man, and I deeply appreciate the hospitality of his home and table on such short notice—"

"But where is your sense of adventure, Hope." Joy's tiny nostrils flared. "I mean...what do you think about him as a man? He's fine, isn't he?"

"Sure, he's handsome." Hope granted. "A very handsome...very married man. If you'll recall, his only comments this evening were about his wife. He's crazy about her—"

"I know that," Joy snapped. "But that may not be for long—"

"Joy!" Her sinister tone sent chills down Hope's spine.

"Well, I'm just saying." Joy shrugged. "I am a hospice nurse; I know these things. His wife...beloved as she may be...is a very sick woman. She's not gonna live forever. Samantha Sterling is full of death; while I, on the other hand, am full of life—"

"Joy—"

"What? I'm simply stating facts...it won't be much longer, and I'm getting my bid in early with the man...to be her replacement—"

"Wha—"

"Afterall, I can take any well woman's man." Joy flipped back her dark curls. "And least of all, a sick one's—"

"Joy?"

"Well, what can I say?" Joy shrugged. "It's always been like this. Men love me, and women hate my guts 'cause they know I can have any man I please—"

"Joy!"

"So, you can just keep your clutchy claws off, Cousin Hope."
Joy bristled. "I've got dibs! I saw him first—"

"Joy, what're you saying? That's a married man—"

"And don't you ever think I've forgotten!" Joy's voice raised an
octave. "I remember that time you had a crush on Butch Ransom—"

"But we were in the eighth grade—"

"Well, I don't care! You had no right! He was mine!"

"Joy...shhh!" Hope cautioned. "You're gonna upset this whole
household—"

"Well, just know this," Joy said, lowering her voice to a whisper,
"Sam is mine—"

"Joy Greene, you know better!" Hope's eyes swirled in disbelief.
"So, let's just change the subject; especially while we're here, sitting
under Mr. and Mrs. Sterling's roof!" She leapt up and removed their
glasses to the kitchen. "After I've washed these, please show me to
my room. I must rebook my flight for tomorrow. It's been a grueling
day...and all of a sudden...I feel very, very tired."

CHAPTER 12

When Hope entered the door to her guestroom on the first floor of the Sterling's home, she was impressed by its sheer beauty. Mrs. Barnes had meticulously provided every conceivable necessity atop the freshly-made bed—plush, colorful towels; a brand-new robe and slippers; and all of the basic toiletries were elegantly displayed. The adjoining bathroom was alive with the flicker of scented candles stationed around the spa tub, which offered a warm, peaceful and welcoming glow. Although everything was top-notch, Hope's hands just could not stop shaking. Joy's coarse remarks after dinner had left her with an uneasy feeling, swirling around in the pit of her gut: "Samantha Sterling is full of death, but I'm full of life."

And this is the same creepy feeling I got the day I overheard our mothers having their secret conversation. They thought I was outside playing, but I was hiding under my mother's bed…listening. And I heard everything they said. Their words scared me then. And they scare me even more, now.

****

"Oh, Faith, I wish everyone would stop telling Joy that she's *the pretty one*," Joy's mother said as she confided her concerns to my mother. "It's all going to her head. It's making her incorrigible—"

"Well, let's face it, Grace. Your daughter is a very pretty girl," my mother said, trying to allay her fears.

"Oh, I know," Joy's mom agreed, "but all of this undue attention is ruining her. I can hardly reach her anymore…even when I threaten to spank her—"

"Surely, it can't be as bad as all that," my mother said. "Joy has always been such a bright and lovely child—"

"But it is as bad as all that, Faith; I promise you. You just don't understand!" Joy's mother finally broke down into tears.

"C'mon, now, Grace. You're my twin sister and my very best friend. What is it? You know you can tell me anything—"

"Oh, Faith...I saw Joy push Hope down to the ground with my own eyes. She gave her a bloody knee simply because she wanted to ride her bike—"

"Well, kids will be kids, Grace, and they are only 10 years old—"

"Yes, but when I called Joy on it, she said, 'It was Hope's fault! She should've given me the bike when I told her to! Besides, she'll be alright. She can take it. She's the big one...the ugly one. Uncle Jude said so.'"

"Our little Joy said that to you?" My mom gasped. "But there's no telling what nonsense her Uncle Jude has been pumping into her head. He is family, but he's a real piece o' work! He's nothing at all like our husbands—"

"Yes, she said it!" Joy's mom sobbed bitterly. "And that's not the worst of it—"

"What is it, sis...tell me...tell me—"

"This is so hard to say. I haven't even had the heart to tell my own husband—"

"Grace, what could be so bad—"

"Joy...my little darling, Joy...fed her canary...to the cat—"

"She did what?!?"

"Yes, Joy killed that bird on purpose!" Her mom sniffed. "Of course, she denied it at first. But when I quizzed her more closely, she finally broke down. She said, 'Yes, I did it! Sure, I did it! I just wanted to see what would happen. And besides, Mommy, why do you care? It wasn't your bird. It was my bird, and it was getting old, squawking, and getting on my nerves. So, I put it out of its misery!'"

"Joy...said that to you?"

"Yes, she did…in those very words…and she showed not a shred of shame…no guilt…no remorse…no pity…nothing—"

"Well, as her mother, I know you must be very concerned. But Joy is my one and only niece, too, and I love her dearly. She's still young. Surely, with time, she'll grow out of it—"

"I sure hope you're right, Faith—"

"C'mon, Grace, we'll do what sisters and mothers have done since the beginning of time. We'll get on our knees; we'll pray about it…right here, right now…together."

And they did. I heard them as I sat paralyzed under that bed. My mother and her beloved twin sister cried their eyes out and prayed for Joy…together.

****

Meanwhile, on the family level upstairs, Joy was in her bedroom, stomping down the carpet in her pink satin slippers and muttering to herself aloud. "The nerve of that Hope! Getting here over two hours late for lunch! How in the world do you get lost between Atlanta and Sandywood, Georgia; it's only 100 miles?!? Nobody asked her to dinner! Nobody invited her to stay the night! I never meant for her to meet Sam…my Sam! But she's always been so unreliable! And what must Sam think…of me…of us…of my entire family…after meeting Hope?!?

Twin cousins…ha! Hope is nothing like me. She's so unrefined… so unaccomplished…so little to offer. And it's not enough that she's not as pretty as me, but she still insists on wearing that nappy-headed natural; even though, from what I hear, she's a pretty fair hair stylist back home. Well, at least she didn't tell Sam that all she does is operate that little, third-rate beauty salon in Kansas City. *O-M-G!* Especially since she could've been so much more…but Hope never bothered to finish college, and it really shows! And she could've finished…right alongside me. But, no! Not Hope! She's never been

77

willing to grind for what she really wants. She's so squeamish…so unimaginative. She's just one, big wuss! She lets the least little thing upset her confidence and drive her off course…like when we were back in Nashville…during our freshman year at Fisk. If only she had listened to me, our lives would be so much different now…so much better—"

****

"Hope! What on earth are you doing?" I can remember pleading with her in our dorm room.

"I'm leaving!" Hope said to me. She was snorting, crying, and flinging her clothes into her luggage like she'd lost her mind.

"What do you mean you're leaving, Hope?" I agonized. "We're just freshmen. We just got here! You can't go home, not now—"

"But I have no choice—"

"Why? Are you crazy? You told me yesterday you were gonna get yourself together…get more involved in campus life…learn the ropes. And you said you were going to that frat party last night so you could meet some new people—"

"But I did go—"

"Then, what's wrong?!?"

"Tyson…Tyson tried to rape me—"

"Tyson Dunn? Tyson Dunn…*Mr. Big-Man-On-Campus*? Tyson Dunn…*The Dean of Pledgees*? Tyson Dunn…*The honor student who can have any pretty girl on this campus he wants*? Why in the world would he ever try to rape you? Hope, you're not making sense—"

"I dunno…but he did! And I'm leaving—"

"But what did he do?"

"Well, we were dancing downstairs…and the music was so loud. And Tyson said for us to go upstairs and talk so we could hear each other better. And I agreed—"

"What?!? You fell for that? That's the lamest old line in the books—"

"He sounded sincere, and I really did want to hear what he had to say—"

"And then what?"

"And, so, we talked...for a while...but then—"

"Then?"

"Then...he pushed me down on the bed and tried to kiss me—"

"But he was just trying to make out with you, Hope; that's not rape—"

"But you just don't understand, Joy. He pushed me down onto the bed...hard...and I felt...so small...so helpless. I couldn't move; I couldn't scream; I couldn't breathe—"

"So, what did you do?"

"I fought him off...and I ran. I ran downstairs. I ran outta the frat house. I ran and everybody was laughing at me—"

"And I don't blame them!" I raged. "You probably looked like a lunatic running outta there when nobody was chasing you—"

"And, now, I can't face them...not Tyson...none of 'em." Hope balled up her sweaters and pitched them into her luggage. "I'm going back to Kansas City where I belong!"

"But, Hope, we've got a great opportunity here! We can become the brilliant doctor and nurse duo we've always dreamed of. Besides, what can you possibly do in Kansas City—"

"I don't know, but I'll find something. I'll get a job in the factory like my daddy—"

"But how will it make me look, Hope?" I screeched to the top of my lungs. "Have you ever considered that? Everybody knows you're my roommate...my cousin...my twin cousin...and all of your stupid mistakes will roll down hill on me!"

"But everybody loves you, Joy. They'll forgive you...but not me. I'm going back home—"

"Oh, Hope! Please, don't go!" I cried; I pled; I raged! "But there was absolutely no reasoning with her."

****

Oh, Hope! Why? Joy dropped to her bedroom floor and flailed her angry fists against the pale carpet. *Why did you run away from your future...our future? We were going to be the medical team that set the whole world on its ear! But you're such a coward...such a loser...such an absolute weenie!!*

Joy rebounded to her feet, swung back her pretty hair, and regained her composure. *So, Hope, I don't know why you never reached your full potential...but I'm not about to let you come in here and mess up my good thing! Not on your life! Not when I'm so close to having everything I've ever wanted...a husband, a home, an absolutely incredible future! So, please, Hope! Leave! Run on back home where you belong. You had your chance. Now, it's my time!!*

CHAPTER 13

"Oh, hi, Joy," Samantha said brightly, forcing her bleary eyes to focus on her nurse as she entered her bedroom. "So...I understand your cousin, Hope, spent last evening with us—"

"Sam told you, huh?" Joy said.

"Well, of course, he did. Sam tells me everything." Samantha's attempt at a fun giggle collapsed into a coarse wheeze. "Did you and Hope have a good visit? Was everything to your liking?"

"Yes." Joy grimaced under her face mask. "Dinner with Sam was delightful, and Mrs. Barnes made us the perfect brunch this morning. We sent Hope back to Atlanta in grand, southern style. Her flight leaves out later today."

"Well, that was perfect timing." Samantha smiled. "I'm glad you got to visit with a member of your own family while you're here. In fact, Sam tells me that the two of you have a special bond. You're not just cousins; you're actually *twin cousins*, right?"

"That's what they tell us," Joy muttered as she applied the blood pressure monitor to Samantha's arm. "But that's a long story from a long time ago."

"Well, you'll have to share it with me—"

"Sure," Joy snipped. "But if you're feeling up to it today, I'd like to talk to you about more important matters—"

"Sounds serious." Samantha's blood pressure spiked.

"Not really, but it does require your immediate attention," Joy said, tucking away the monitor. "It's about the expansion plans for the church's Soup Kitchen."

"Oh, yes," Samantha said, "Sam did tell me that you'd given him an update on your recent meeting with Pastor Jamie—"

"Oh, did he, now?"

"Yes, he did." A sly smile tickled at the corners of Samantha's mouth. She was delighted to be kept up-to-date with the movements in her household.

"Then I guess Sam told you that Pastor Jamie gave me a grand tour of the entire operation last Sunday—"

"Yes, he did—"

"And, I must say, everything is very impressive—"

"Thank you." Samantha's smile broadened. "We've worked very hard to make it a wonderful experience for everyone who comes. We want everyone who enters our doors to feel welcomed, to feel loved, and to feel like our honored guests—"

"And Pastor Jamie showed me what remains to be done, and it looks like a really big job."

"Yes, there's always room for improvement—"

"And did Sam tell you how very excited Pastor Jamie is with my new idea?"

"What idea is that, Joy?"

"My idea is to contact the contractors who can handle the sound system upgrades, so I can negotiate the best price—"

"Oh, yes, Sam did mention that, but—"

"Well, I can contact some prime contractors nearby…and maybe some in Atlanta…and get them to work together as a team to provide the services we need. And if they work together, they may be able to shave off some of the costs and pass the savings on to us. So, the church can stay on budget—"

"Oh, you mean…form a consortium of contractors who are able to achieve economies of scale that will offer cost-cutting measures to keep us within budget—"

"Yes, that's what I said." Joy sniffed. "If I can get four or five of them working together, they may be able to find ways to give us a better price—"

"And you'll be taking the lead?"

"Yes, of course." Joy bristled. "I've already told the pastor and Sam that I plan to start contacting contractors right away—"

"That's all very interesting." Samantha wheezed. "But as I was attempting to say to you earlier…Sam reminded me that I've already had a similar idea…some time ago." She braced on her bed table to catch her breath. "And I've already compiled a comprehensive list of contractors who might be able and willing to work with us—"

"Is that so?" Joy's tiny nostrils flared.

"Well, didn't Sam tell you about my list?" Samantha replied, but her confident smile flattened into a craggy cough. "I just haven't had the energy to reach out to any of the firms as of yet." She cleared her throat. "So, Joy, if you'd like to do that, I'll print you a copy of my resource list. And that way, you won't have to reinvent the wheel by developing a list of your own—"

"Sure." Joy rocked impatiently. "I guess that could be helpful—"

"And I can assure you, Joy; the list is quite extensive." Samantha sparkled. "In addition to providing the company's name with their particular specialty, I've also added the primary contact person and their current contact information—"

"Well, I guess that'll be a start." Joy granted.

"But…but I don't think I can get over to my computer today," Samantha said after being unable to move her legs to the side of her bed. "So, if you'll set my computer up right here on my bed table, I can get that list for you—"

"Sure," Joy said, making a mental note of Samantha's several failed attempts to get out of bed. She retrieved the computer from its sunny corner and plopped it onto Samantha's bed table.

"Here's the list," Samantha said triumphantly after logging in to upload her file. "I'll just hit print, and the list should spit out in just a minute.

"Got it," Joy said when the three-page document emerged. "So, this is it—"

"Good deal," Samantha said. "Hopefully, that'll save you some extra legwork. And as a side note, I've already put a blue dot next to the companies that I think would work best together based on their particular specialties—"

"Noted."

"And, of course, I'm looking forward to hearing what kind of reaction you get from all the companies—"

"I'll be moving rather fast…but, sure, I'll try to keep you in the loop when I can."

"And since we're a charity and a non-profit, I hope the responses you receive will be very favorable—"

"What's wrong?" Joy refocused her attention.

"Don't know—" Samantha's breath quickened. "Don't seem to be able to move my fingers… my right hand isn't working. Can't log out…never happened before…never—"

"Hold on; I'll do it for you," Joy said, logging off the computer. "Now, can you squeeze my hand?"

"No." Samantha's voice trembled with anxiety. "I…I can't—"

"Calm down," Joy said. "It's probably just a temporary spasm. Maybe, it's a minor side-effect of the new drugs; or, just maybe, this whole church project is getting to be too much for you, Samantha—"

"Oh-h, Joy, I'm…so scared." Samantha hyperventilated. "Call Sam—"

"No, we shouldn't trouble Sam right now. He's very busy—"

"Then let Dr. Wallace know—"

"Dr. Wallace will be here on Monday, Samantha. I'm sure you'll be just fine until then—"

"Well, if I forget…if I forget to tell him…please tell the doctor for me, Joy…please—"

"Of course, I will, Samantha," Joy said with a syrupy grin. "And I'm certain Dr. Wallace will be able to fix you right up. But in the meantime, you need to relax. Just lie back, close your eyes, and get yourself some much-needed rest. I've got everything in hand, and

everything is going to be much better soon. I can promise you that."
Um-hmm! Yes, indeedy, Mrs. Sterling...real soon!

CHAPTER 14

By the time Dr. Wallace arrived for his scheduled visit on Monday, Samantha's right hand was back to normal. In fact, Sam was holding the very hand that had gone rogue when the doctor entered her room. "Well, how are you today, my dear?" Dr. Wallace smiled at his favorite patient. "Has everything been going well?"

"Well, I'm fine as a fiddle, except for a few hiccups along the way," Samantha said spiritedly. "And, now, I can't even remember what they were."

"That's great news," Dr. Wallace said. "I've had no reports of serious problems from Nurse Greene, and she's my eyes and ears—"

"No new problems to report, doctor," Joy said crisply, although she was acutely aware that the weakness in Samantha's right hand a few days earlier—and her inability to get out of bed on her own— were very abnormal occurrences.

"I've been monitoring your vitals remotely, and Nurse Green has been shipping me your blood samples. And by all accounts, things are looking as well as expected. Has your energy level improved? I know that was a concern for you on my last visit."

"I—" Samantha's eyes flickered wildly as she struggled to find her words. "I—"

"Samantha?" Sam dropped her right hand that had suddenly gone limp. "Samantha! Samantha, what's wrong? What's the matter?"

"Nurse Greene, pass me my stethoscope!" the doctor barked. "Hurry!"

"Dr. Wallace, what's wrong?!?" Sam begged. "What's wrong with my wife—"

"I think she's fainted," Dr. Wallace said. "Nurse Greene, get some cold compresses…immediately!"

When Samantha finally revived, she tried to speak. Her lips were moving frantically, but she could not make a sound. Her eyes were wide open, and they were flooded with panic.

"I think she may have suffered a mild stroke," Dr. Wallace said after examining Samantha.

"Then let's do something!" Sam screeched. "Let's hurry and get an ambulance! Let's get her to the nearest hospital!"

"Sam…Sam," Dr. Wallace said consolingly. "I don't think that would do any good. Samantha is waning—"

"No! No!" Sam screamed to the top of his lungs. "That can't be! Not Samantha…my Samantha!"

"We can keep her comfortable…but that's about all we'll be able do—"

"I can't accept that! I won't accept that!" Sam wailed. "Her eyes are moving. She's looking right at me. She can see me—"

"Yes, she can see you, Sam," Dr. Wallace said quietly, "and, yes, she can hear you. But at this stage of her disease progression, we can't reverse the more harmful effects that the stroke might've caused…and those effects may be permanent—"

"Loss of speech? It can't be! No! No way! I must be able to talk to Samantha. We must be able to talk to each other—"

"You will be able to talk to Samantha, Sam. And she may be able to understand you…but she may not be able to speak to you—"

"No! Sam wailed with his head in his hands. "God! No!"

After he'd settled his patient, Dr. Wallace quietly removed the tubing from Samantha's port and whispered his new orders. "Nurse Greene, I'm taking Mrs. Sterling off of all of the new intravenous chemo drugs. They don't appear to be helping, and the side-effects are too unpredictable. I'm prescribing a mild sedative to keep her comfortable until we can determine the extent of the damage from this latest episode."

"Yes, Doctor," Joy said crisply. "I understand."

In all of the commotion, Mrs. Barnes had flown up from the kitchen, expecting the worst. She collapsed against the doorway to Samantha's room. *Oh, thank God! Mrs. Sterling's still here...but look at her. She's just lying there, looking all weak and pitiful. My heart goes out to Mr. Sterling...but there's nothing I can do. There's nothing anybody can do, but the Lord. Oh, Lord, my dear Lord, please...please help Mrs. Sterling!*

CHAPTER 15

The next day, when everyone was out of the room, Joy whipped off her mask and leaned down beside Samantha's bed. She allowed her long, dark curls to flop onto Samantha's face, and she whispered directly into her incapacitated patient's ear. "I guess it doesn't matter anymore whether I wear this mask or not because a virus is the least of your worries, Missy. In fact, in your failing health, Samantha, nothing really matters anymore. You're losing your grip…your grip on life…your grip on sanity…your grip on everything you hold dear. Ha! But I want to set your mind at ease, dear heart. You don't have to worry anymore. From now on, I will be taking over your prized project at the church. I will be working directly with Pastor Jamie. I will be taking over your beautiful home. And, most of all, I will be taking over your f-i-n-e husband. I'm biding my time with him for now; but make no mistake, Missy, he will be mine. All of his millions will be mine. His heart will be mine, and I will make him happier than you ever could. In fact, everything you've ever considered to be yours, Samantha Sterling, will soon be mine. So, my dear, please feel free to go ahead and die…and the sooner, the better—"

"Grrrr!" Samantha's throat vibrated with a guttural growl, and her body twitched violently in response to Joy's mean words; but she was unable to utter a word. She couldn't move her lips. She couldn't move her body. She could only move her eyes, and they were flashing like emergency strobe lamps.

"How's my beautiful bride today?" Sam said as he eased into Samantha's room, and Joy fumbled clumsily to reseat her face mask.

"Unfortunately, no changes to report," Joy stuttered. "But, Sam, you're looking so tired. Are you getting enough rest? You know it's important for you—"

"I'm fine," Sam snapped and moved over to his wife's bedside. When he reached for her limp right hand, he noticed that Samantha's eyes were swirling wildly. Unbeknownst to him, she was still reeling from her encounter with Joy. "Baby," Sam said, "what's wrong? Are you in pain?" Samantha made every effort to calm the agitation in her eyes so she could blink more purposefully.

"Look at that!" Sam cheered. "I told you! Samantha can hear me, and she's trying to speak to me—"

"But based on her prognosis, Sam, I'm afraid that would be impossible—"

"Not with her voice," Sam growled, "but with her eyes—"

"But, Sam, that's medically impossible—"

"I've known Samantha most of my life, Nurse Greene, and I know when my wife is speaking to me—"

"But—"

"I wish she could use her hands," Sam said, "then she could write down what she's trying to say—"

"But she can't—"

"I know that's the case right now." Sam fumed. "But, maybe, there's something we can do to strengthen her right hand so she can hold a pen—"

"There's not—"

"Samantha," Sam said, looking directly into her eyes, "can you hear me, baby?"

Samantha struggled to regain her composure, and she blinked her eyes…once. She wanted her eyes to speak all of the words she so desperately needed to say in order to protect her beloved husband. She wanted Sam to know all of the vile things that Joy had said. She wanted to warn him of the depravity of her wicked plan.

"See, Joy, I told you she can hear me," Sam said hopefully.

"Well, Dr. Wallace said she may be able to hear…but she can never respond—"

"Samantha, baby, if you understand me, will you blink your eyes again for me…once for *yes* and twice for *no*?" Sam waited; and slowly, Samantha responded. She blinked her eyes once, and then she blinked them twice as requested. "Joy, she's doing it!" Sam exclaimed joyfully.

"I see—" Joy's eyes flashed in dismay.

"Samantha, would you like some water?" Sam said, and his wife blinked once, *yes*. Sam retrieved her favorite butterfly water bottle from the bedside table and placed the straw to her lips. Samantha's eyes smiled at her husband, and she took a sip.

"See!" Sam said ecstatically.

"Yes, but—" Joy's body froze.

"Come on, Samantha," Sam said. "Let's try it, again…once for *yes* and twice for *no*—"

"Sam," Joy protested, "you're tiring my patient, and she needs her rest—"

"Maybe, you're right," Sam conceded after Samantha finally closed her eyes. "But I will keep trying. I know she can do it; she's just too tired to focus right now."

"Well, maybe there's something Dr. Wallace can do to make communication between the two of you possible." *Ha! Fat chance!* "Would you like for me to call him?"

"No, Joy, thank you." Sam measured his words, attempting to camouflage his annoyance with her persistent negativity. "I'll speak with him myself."

"Yes, Sam, I think that's a great idea." Joy said, moving close enough for him to feel her body heat and smell her expensive perfume. "But in the meantime, if there's anything I can do for you, Sam…anything at all—"

"No, Nurse Greene, I can't think of a thing," Sam said as he took a deliberate step away from her advances. "In fact, I'll go downstairs right now and call Dr. Wallace. I'm sure he'll be happy to hear of Samantha's progress."

As soon as Sam descended on the elevator, Joy swooped back down on Samantha's bedside like a greedy vulture. She removed her mask and buzzed close to her patient's ear. "Good try, Missy, but good ain't good enough! What good is *yes* or *no* if Sam doesn't know the right questions to ask, huh? Your eyes can tell no tales, Missy, so you might as well go ahead and close them for the very last time…and at your earliest convenience, p-lease. You haven't got a prayer, Samantha. And nobody can help you now!"

CHAPTER 16

"Mr. Sterling," Mrs. Barnes said, easing her heavy frame into the doorway of his private office, "you can't keep this up—"

"What?" Sam said. He was crouched over his acrylic desk, head in hands.

"It's been nearly a month since Mrs. Sterling had that li'l ole stroke. And all you do is worry about her all day and work yourself to a frazzle every night. You can't keep this up! You're gonna make yo'self sick, and that won't help yo' wife none."

"I know, Mrs. Barnes." Sam raised his head. "But in all this time, Samantha's only been able to blink her eyes to respond to me. She can't do much more than that, and I want to talk to my wife. I need to hear her voice again. I'm really worried about her, but what can I do?"

"Pray." Mrs. Barnes firmed. "Yeah, they say her recovery is 'medically impossible', Mr. Sterling, and it very well might be. But we know our Father has never lost a case; and He hears us when we go to Him in earnest prayer. So, you can pray right along with the rest of us. Pastor Jamie has got the whole church praying for Mrs. Sterling and for you, and we're all believing God for a miracle—"

"But I do pray—"

"I know you do. But you still can't stay cooped up inside this house...with the blinds drawn. It ain't good for you, Mr. Sterling. You need to get outside. Get you some fresh air and sunshine—"

"The interior blinds are open, Mrs. Barnes—"

"I see that; but you need to open these exterior blinds, so you can get some full sun," Mrs. Barnes said, busying herself to do just that. But when the exterior blinds swung open, what she saw was Joy—in full flesh—sunbathing by the pool. Her legs were long and sleek, her skin flawless. She was slathered in body oil and twisting and turning on the lounge chair like she was on a rotisserie. All of her assets were showing in a skimpy, rose-colored bikini, and it was obvious Joy thought Sam could see her from his office window. However, there was no way she could've known about the double set of blinds. And immediately, Mrs. Barnes fully understood why Sam kept the exterior blinds closed. *Hmm? I wonder how many times Nurse Joy pulled this stunt before Mr. Sterling got wise and shut the blinds?*

"I know...you're right, Mrs. Barnes," Sam said, swiveling his desk chair away from the window. "I know I should get out more—"

"Yes, siree!" Mrs. Barnes said as she quickly retraced her steps and snapped the exterior blinds shut. "You gotta get up outta this house. And you gotta go talk to somebody...somebody who loves you...somebody who understands...somebody who can pray yo' strength in the Lord—"

"And who might that be, Mrs. Barnes—"

"Tell you what," Mrs. Barnes said brightly. "Get up right now and go over to the church and talk to Pastor Jamie. I know he'd be glad to see you. He'd stop by here, but he just doesn't wanna be under foot. But if you were to go over to the church, you could sit and talk with him. I know he'd love that—"

"But what if Samantha should need me?"

"Mrs. Sterling is fine. She's got Nurse Greene with her 'round the clock. That is...when she ain't lollygagging by the pool. And, of course, I'm here if either of them should need me. So, go and let yo' mind run free, Mr. Sterling. Go see 'bout yo'self. Go talk to Pastor and hear what he's gotta say."

"Alright, Mrs. Barnes," Sam said. "You know I really value your opinion...and most of all, I covet your prayers—"

"I know you do, Mr. Sterling. You're like the *Number-One* son I never had." Mrs. Barnes turned back toward the kitchen. "Now, get outta here and go have some man-talk with Pastor."

****

"Come in, Sam! Come in!" Pastor Jamie drew Sam into a bear hug and pounded his back. He'd been delighted to get his call, and he'd cleared his schedule immediately to meet with him. "I wore my extra-special mask," the pastor said, "so we could get up-close and personal."

"Me, too." Sam chuckled. "And it is so good to see you, Pastor Jamie—"

"Yes, indeed, my brother," the pastor said. "The Lord teaches brotherly love because He knows we're gonna need each other in this life...especially in trying times like these—"

"Yes, Lord!" Sam took a seat across from his desk. "I'm sorry I've been so...out of touch...but I've been so concerned about Samantha—"

"No need to apologize." Pastor Jamie nodded kindly and pushed his blonde locks behind his ears. "Mrs. Barnes has been keeping us posted on everything...and man, she's been praying and having all of us pray, too. That woman is truly a prayer warrior—"

"Yes, Pastor, I know she is, and I'm so glad God sent her to be on our side."

"Me, too," Pastor Jamie tugged on his mask. "But what of you, Sam? How're you holding up?"

"Oh, I don't know how I feel from one minute to the next." Sam's head drooped. "I'm so thankful Samantha's still alive, and she's got a fighting chance. You know, she's able to communicate with me with her eyes, now...but that's about all. The doctor is keeping her sedated and comfortable, and Nurse Greene is with her 24-7."

"Yes, Nurse Greene." Pastor Jamie's eyes flashed. "I just don't know how she finds the time to do all that she's doing for our church—"

"Oh—"

"Yes," the pastor said, "Joy has been an angel in disguise to this church. She has been working for weeks to assemble a team of contractors to complete the sound system upgrades in the Soup Kitchen, and I am so impressed with her diligence—"

"How so?"

"Well, didn't she tell you?"

"No…at least, not yet. There's little time for much else now than caring for Samantha—"

"Well, Joy must be inventing time because she's just about got this project licked—"

"Really?"

"Yes, she's single-handedly assembled a top-notch team of contractors for the project; and they have all but agreed to all of our terms; and they promise to bring the project in on schedule…and under budget—"

"Wow! Great news! I'm sure Samantha will be so pleased!"

"Yes, I tell you Sam, Joy has done a commendable job and in such a short time. She's been hosting Zoom meetings with me and the committee, and she's been so easy to work with. Everybody says so. Maybe, she's doing it as a tribute to you and Samantha…to set your minds at ease during this troubling time. That's not to say she could ever fill Samantha's shoes, but she has been working really hard to give it her all—"

"Well, I'm really glad to hear that—"

"I know you must be delighted to have Joy working on your team, too…with Samantha's care, I mean."

"Yes, Pastor, I don't know what we would do without her. Before the stroke, Samantha said how grateful she was for Joy's care. And even now, when Joy is nearby, Samantha's eyes blaze in her direction. Although, whenever I'm with Samantha, Joy seems to keep her distance. I guess she wants to respect our privacy and our most precious time together. So, yes, Pastor, Joy has been fantastic to Samantha…and to me—"

"Oh?"

"Well…she is a trusted member of our household…kind and considerate…and she seems to care a lot about my welfare, as well—"

"And…she is quite a beautiful young lady—"

"That might be so, Pastor, but that's not my concern—"

"Oh, I know, Sam…but you never know what the future might hold—"

"Future?" Sam's eyes flashed in disbelief. "Pastor, all I can think about is Samantha getting well—"

"Of course…forgive me for even suggesting—" Pastor Jamie paused abruptly for the knock at his door. "And Sam, since I knew you were stopping by, I've got a special treat for you—"

"What?"

"Not what…who." The pastor swung open his door.

"Chief?" Sam startled. "What're you doing here?"

"Glad you can recognize me behind this big ole mask," Chief of Police Rufus Outlaw teased as he added a hearty laugh. He was standing erectly in full uniform—including his 10-gallon hat—and hoisting a fistful of greasy brown paper bags. "I was called into service 'cause you're my good brother, and we need good food—"

"Yes," the pastor said, adding an agreeable nod, "physical food and spiritual food!"

"But I almost couldn't break away," the Chief admitted. "We've been having such a devil of a time with our County Coroner…that Buster Clayton! He wouldn't even be our coroner if his uncle wasn't the Chief Medical Examiner for the state. And if you ask me, nepotism never works. Just look at what's happened at the White House—"

"Well, we're glad you were able make it," Pastor Jamie said, "because I want us to have a chance to pray together. I know you trust Chief Outlaw, Sam. And the Lord promises that where two or three are gathered together in His name, He'll be in our midst—"

"And if that right there ain't enough convincing for you," the chief guffawed, "I brought the ribs! So, after we pray, we can 'rise-Peter-slay-and-eat'—"

"Yesiree! These good ole country sayings are certainly apropos." Pastor Jamie chuckled. "So, spiritual food first…and then, physical food—"

"Ahh, brothers," Sam said, humbled by their genuine care and concern, "you two are truly the best. And I can't tell you how much I needed this. Nothing like believers pressing the flesh. Thanks to both of you—"

"Sam, we…in fact, the whole, entire church…we've all missed you and Samantha so much!" the chief said as he tossed his big hat aside and stashed the mouth-watering, southern-styled barbeque on a back table.

"So—" Pastor Jamie said, standing and clasping hands with Sam Sterling and Rufus Outlaw. "Brothers, let us pray!"

CHAPTER 17

"Well, good morning, Dr. Wallace," Mrs. Barnes said, greeting him warmly at the front door of the Sterling's residence. It was a glorious Monday morning, and Dr. Wallace had arrived right on schedule for his weekly appointment. "I'm sure you can find your way upstairs."

"Thank you, Mrs. Barnes," the doctor said. "I'll go right up after I've washed up down here."

"Sure thing." Mrs. Barnes smiled. "I'll let Mr. Sterling know you're here."

"Good morning, Nurse Greene," Dr. Wallace greeted warmly as he entered his patient's room. "And how is Mrs. Sterling...that is, Samantha...this morning?"

"Good morning, Doctor," Joy said crisply. "I have nothing new to report. Samantha's vital signs are stable."

"That's good to hear," Dr. Wallace said, moving to her bedside. Her eyes were wide open and alert with eagerness. "Good morning, Samantha, can you hear me?" Samantha blinked once for *yes*. "I'm glad to see you're still communicating with your eyes," the doctor said. "I'm going to touch you in a number of places this morning to gauge your responses. When I ask you, I want you to let me know if you're able to feel my touch. Do you understand?" Samantha's eyes blinked, *yes*. "Okay, that's good. Now, let's begin."

When Sam entered the room, Joy grabbed his arm and pulled him over closer to her side. "Dr. Wallace is probing to determine Samantha's responses," she whispered. "You can stand with me and watch from here—"

"No, thank you, Joy; I'd rather join the doctor," Sam said as he avoided her touch and moved over to his wife's bedside.

"Samantha, Sam has joined us," Dr. Wallace said. "Can you see him?" Samantha's eyes warmed and blinked once for *yes*."

"Hey there, baby," Sam said, "how're you feeling this morning? Good?" Samantha's face curled into a crooked smile, and her eyes blinked once more for *yes*.

"I'm touching you on your left foot right now," Dr. Wallace said. "Samantha, are you able to feel that?" Samantha's eyes dimmed, and she blinked twice for *no*.

"That's okay, baby, don't be alarmed," Sam encouraged. "I love you—"

And from out of what seemed to be a bottomless pit, Samantha's voice rose to say, "L—ove you—"

"What?" Dr. Wallace's tools bobbled in his hands. "Samantha, can you say it again?"

"L—ove," Samantha repeated.

"That's beautiful, baby," Sam said, kissing her right hand, over and over again.

"Well, can you feel this?" Dr. Wallace passed his probe across Samantha's lips. She blinked once for *yes*, and she attempted to nod her head.

"Yes!" Sam raved. "My baby has come back to me! She's come back to me!"

"S—am—"

"Yes, baby! Yes, baby! I'm right here—"

"J—oy—" Samantha's voice growled and scalding tears formed in her eyes; but in all of the excitement, no one noticed her intense agitation. She ached to tell Sam the truth about Joy's wicked plans, but she had no way of making her beloved husband understand.

"Don't worry, Samantha," Sam said, "Joy is right here with us, too—"

"What's going on?" Mrs. Barnes said as she bypassed Joy who was splattered out across the door frame like a pancake.

"She's talking! She's talking!" Sam cheered. "Mrs. Barnes, my baby is speaking to me, again—"

"Praise Jesus!" Mrs. Barnes exclaimed. "It had to happen; the whole church's been praying, and the Lord done heard our cries! Glory be…His Name be praised!"

"It's a medical miracle, all right," Dr. Wallace said, scratching his head. "It surely must be!"

"Uggh!" Nurse Greene clasped her hand over her mouth to stifle her anguished cry. And in all of the commotion, she crept into the hallway and plastered her back against the rear wall. She felt faint. Her knees were weak. She was rocky on her feet. "Oh, no! This can't be! What if she really starts talking again? What if she becomes able to tell Sam…everything…every mean thing I've ever said to her? Oh, no! It can't be! It can never be! I'll be ruined! Wh—what am I gonna do?"

CHAPTER 18

Dr. Wallace had been so elated and encouraged by Samantha's breakthrough on his Monday visit that he'd left new orders for her continuing care. He'd reduced the dosage of her sedative, and he'd added a new, state-of-the-art anti-inflammatory drug. And as he was leaving, he'd given Joy his final instructions. "Nurse Greene, if we can reduce the inflammation, it could very well reverse some of the nerve damage in Samantha's extremities. And if we get her limbs moving again," the doctor said excitedly, "we may be able to get her up and walking...and writing. That would allow her to communicate better with her husband. Wouldn't that be great?"

"Yes, of course, Doctor," Joy said, grateful that her face mask was hiding her grave displeasure. *Sure thing, Doc! Now, wouldn't that be just peachy-keen?!?*

But on the following day, on Tuesday, Joy was left alone with Samantha for most of the day. Sam had been called away to the West Coast for an emergency meeting with his staff. Their latest project was at a critical stage, and there was no margin for error. Since the stakes were so high, a face-to-face meeting couldn't be avoided. So, Sam said his sweet good-byes to Samantha on the previous evening, and he promised to return in three days—tops.

When Mrs. Barnes came and went with Samantha's breakfast tray on that Tuesday morning, Joy locked the bedroom door and pulled a side chair up close to Samantha's bedside. "So," Joy said in a coarse whisper, "we're trying to talk now; are we?" Her hot breath slathered across Samantha's fragile face. Samantha struggled to turn her head aside, but Joy forced it back in her direction. "You had me scared there for a minute, Missy, but you can just give up on this talking notion. It ain't gonna happen! I have already told you what's gonna happen, and you should've just been a good, little girl and accepted the inevitable...just let things be. But, no-o, you're trying to talk! You're trying to ruin my carefully laid plans...and you know I cannot let that slide!" Joy's voice flamed. "But what you didn't know is I've been adding some of my own special, super-duper elixir to your prized butterfly water bottle every day. Oh, don't worry. It's odorless, colorless, tasteless. No one will ever know. But even that didn't seem to shut you up!"

"S—am—" Samantha pleaded from her innermost being.

"Sam? Sam can't help you now. He's not here!" Joy spat. "You may be able to call his name, but you're not smart enough anymore to string three words together, least of all a complete sentence. So, how do you think you're gonna tell Sam what I've got in store for him, hmm?" Joy's words blazed through her knotted lips. "Let's face it! You can't! And, now, you've left me no choice. I can't chance it...not anymore. Dr. Wallace wants me to cut your sedation, but I'm gonna double it. Dr. Wallace wants to give you anti-inflammatory drugs, but I'm gonna flush 'em right down the toilet. Dr. Wallace wants you to get better, but I want you dead! You're sick, Samantha. You're tired, Samantha. You're ugly, Samantha. You're in my way, Samantha—" Joy's voice suddenly slowed. "And you make me so mad! You've served your purpose. You got me close to Sam. And, now, you've outlived your usefulness. So...I'm not gonna wait! I'm gonna put you out o' your misery! Oh, yes...and I'm gonna do it today—"

"J—esus—" Samantha's tortured body seized.

"That's right, Missy. Make peace with your Maker. 'Cause I've got a cocktail that's gonna set your soul on fire. I always keep a little stash for my terminally-ill patients. A little something just for times like these...when I've grown weary of changing their bedpans, washing their stank butts, and listening to their incessant whining. But for you, dear Samantha, I've done you one better. I've shown you my crystal ball. I've let you see into your future. I've told you how things will be with me and Sam once you're gone. And if you are the bigger woman, as everyone seems to think you are, then that should make you happy…knowing your beloved Sam will be well taken care of as my fabulous, new husband—"

"Ugggh!" Samantha's throat swelled, choking on the words she was no longer able to utter.

While she was speaking, Joy had been preparing an injection and tapping on the needle…*plunk-plunk*. "So, where would you like it, Miss Samantha…this super-duper cocktail of mine? It's a hot-shot of chemo drugs that anyone would expect to find floating around in the system of a dying cancer patient. Well, should we put it in your arm? Behind your knee? Oh, no…let's make it quite impossible for the coroner to find; shall we? Let's put this nice, neat needle prick right here…between your toes. Feel that? Maybe not? But you can relax, now, my dearly-departed Samantha Sterling. It's all over for you. Bye-bye! It won't be long now—"

CHAPTER 19

"Good afternoon, Mrs. Barnes, that smells mighty tasty," Joy said brightly as the housekeeper shuffled into Samantha's room with her dinner tray that evening. "I'm sure Samantha will enjoy it. And since you're here, I think I'll take myself a little break—"

"You do that, Nurse Greene." Mrs. Barnes' lips twirled. "Me and Mrs. Sterling, we'll be just fine—"

"I'm sure you will." Joy's lips tightened under her face mask. "And I'll be right downstairs in the study…if you should need me for anything—"

"Hello, there, Mrs. Sterling," Mrs. Barnes said as she set the tray onto Samantha's bedside table. "I've brought you your favorite this time…chicken and dumplings…and I really hope it's to your liking. So, c'mon now, you've gotta sit up and eat—" Mrs. Barnes gasped, and the silverware tray clanged noisily to the floor. "Mrs. Sterling! Mrs. Sterling! What's wrong, Mrs. Sterling? Nurse Greene! Nurse Greene! Come quick! Come see 'bout Mrs. Sterling! Come now! Right now!"

"What is it?" Joy said as she flew back into the room from where she'd been lurking quietly in the hallway. "What's all the fuss?"

"Check her…check her!" Mrs. Barnes demanded, falling back onto a chair for support. "Check Mrs. Sterling!"

"Oh, Mrs. Barnes," Joy said after pretending to render aid to her patient, "I'm afraid…I'm so very afraid; it's too late. She's…she's already gone—"

"No! No!" Mrs. Barnes wailed to the top of her lungs. "Oh, no, Mrs. Sterling can't be…she can't be…she can't be gone!"

"But I'm afraid she is, Mrs. Barnes," Joy said coolly. "Will you call Sam…or should I?"

"No!" Mrs. Barnes settled herself. "I'll call Mr. Sterling. You call 911…and get the ambulance—"

"But I assure you, Mrs. Barnes; there's nothing they can do," Joy said clinically. "But you are quite right. That is the proper protocol for handling a dead…a deceased…a corpse—"

"Oh, Lord! Oh, no!" Mrs. Barnes wailed as she moved toward the door. "This…right here…this gonna break Mr. Sterling's heart! Po' baby! Po' baby!"

****

The red-eye flight back to Atlanta was agonizing, and the drive back to Sandywood was interminable. Sam was devastated, and it took every ounce of his energy and every fiber of his faith to make the journey. He was driving like a phantom in the night, wading through an impenetrable fog. His headlights cast eerie shadows into the blackness—a bleak reflection of his own somber mood. The lack of heavy traffic and his familiarity with the dangerous back roads were his only saving grace.

Sam dropped his bag by the back door when he entered his house at 3 a.m., and Mrs. Barnes was sitting in the kitchen waiting for him. When he crossed his threshold, she grabbed him into a warm, motherly embrace. "I am so very sorry, Mr. Sterling," Mrs. Barnes said, "so very, very sorry—"

"I know." Sam said, finally giving way to his own sobs. "But there is absolutely nothing we can do for my Samantha, now…it's all in God's hands—"

"You're right." Mrs. Barnes consoled. "Mrs. Sterling is in the presence of her Lord…and all is well—"

"I've…I've got to make the arrangements—"

"But not tonight, Mr. Sterling," Mrs. Barnes said. "I spoke to Pastor Jamie, and he and Chief Outlaw will come 'round first thing this morning and help you make all the arrangements."

"Thank you, Mrs. Barnes. You have always been a rock for our family, and I appreciate you more than you can ever know—"

"Oh, I know, Mr. Sterling, and it's my pleasure. So, c'mon, now. You go upstairs and get you some rest. You're gonna have a big day—"

"Where's Samantha…her body, I mean—"

"The ambulance took it away to the Coroner's Office. You know they've gotta make their review…since she died at home and all—"

"Yes, Mrs. Barnes, I know—"

"Don't stop by your wife's room…not tonight, Mr. Sterling. Get you some rest, now, and you'll be able to bear it better in the light o' day—"

"You're right, of course." Sam squeezed her hand. "Where's Joy?"

"Well, I hope she's up in her room sleeping. She had a very busy night—"

"Of course…I'll speak with her…give her my thanks for all she's done to help my wife…later—"

"That's right; you've done all you can for one night. Good night, sir—"

"Good night, Mrs. Barnes."

****

After breakfast that same morning, Pastor Jamie and Chief Outlaw rang the front door bell at 2200 Bird of Paradise Road. The pastor's head was bowed, and the chief was aimlessly squeezing his big hat in both hands.

"Good morning," Mrs. Barnes greeted the men warmly, "won't you come in? Mr. Sterling is in his wife's room. He's been in there for quite some time. I'll fetch him directly—"

"No, ma'am," Chief Outlaw said. "We ain't in no rush, Mrs. Barnes. We'll just wait right here in the vestibule if that's alright with you—"

"That's right, Sister Barnes," Pastor Jamie echoed kindly, "we're on Sam's timetable today. We'll wait."

"Good morning, brothers," Sam said warmly as he descended the staircase. "Mrs. Barnes told me you were coming. I see you're here bright and early—"

"Well, Sam," Chief Outlaw said, "no time like the present—"

"We just wanted to be able to give you all the time you need, Sam," Pastor Jamie said. "We're at your disposal all day today. You just tell us what you'd like us to do—"

"Well, if you think it wise, Pastor, I think we should go over to the funeral home first and make the arrangements, and then we can see what we need to do from there."

"Sounds like a plan," the chief said. "You just relax and get your thoughts together. I'll drive."

"Thanks," Sam said. "That'll be a big help…and Pastor, I'm sure you'll be able to tell me what the normal protocol is at our church on such occasions. I'll follow your lead at the funeral home."

"Good," Pastor Jamie said. "Let's ride."

The visit to the funeral home was brief. Sam knew that Samantha wouldn't want anything ostentatious. It wasn't her style. Samantha would want something simple. She would want her funeral to be a praise service, heralding the goodness of the Lord. So, Sam picked a simple white coffin with a silk inlay that was covered in golden butterflies. He and the funeral director spent more time discussing the multi-colored, floral arrangement that would blanket her coffin than they did about the program. Sam knew that Samantha would want no pictures and no obituary reciting her life's accomplishments. He could hear her voice in his head, "If they didn't choose to know me by now, baby, it's a little too late; don't you think?"

So, instead, with the pastor's concurrence, Sam settled on a memorial program that would include songs of praise; a brief eulogy to be delivered by the pastor; and after which, the doors of the church would be swung wide open to invite everyone in the audience to accept Jesus Christ as their Lord and to be saved on the spot. That was it. And Sam could hear his wife's sweet voice reverberating in his brain, "And that, my dear husband, is quite enough. Thank you, baby!"

After they left the funeral home, Chief Outlaw drove the trio to the nearest greasy spoon for lunch. "On a day like today, we need to get our carbs on," he said as he swung his top-cop car into a reserved parking spot. "And, Sam, I do apologize. I thought it had already been handled. It should've been handled." The chief rattled on. "I thought the funeral home would've had Samantha's body by now, but this coroner of ours has been giving everybody the blues. He's stuck us with a backlog you can-not imagine! I don't know if Buster Clayton is incompetent or just plain lazy. But fortunately, this is his last week on the job before the new coroner comes on board. And trust me; everybody at the courthouse will be glad to see Buster go. Good riddance! And, Sam, I'll also see to it that Samantha's body is released to the funeral home as quickly as possible—"

"Oh, I know you will, Chief," Sam said. "No worries; it'll all get sorted out in due course. And I guess...I'd rather see Samantha after the funeral home has done its magic—"

"You've got it!" the chief said. "And thank you so much for your understanding—"

"Let's eat," the pastor said, and they all nodded their agreement. The waitress took their orders for their favorite items—greasy and piping hot off the grill—and they settled in for some serious talk.

"Sam," Pastor Jamie remarked, "if I may say so...you appear to be handling things quite well—"

"You think?"

"Yeah, for it being all sudden like," Chief Outlaw said, "I really do. I was braced for you to be a basket case this morning—"

"I echo the point," the pastor agreed. "But I'm glad we could be here to support you."

"Well, to tell the truth," Sam said, folding his hands, "I guess I was headed for a meltdown, but—"

"But?"

"Pastor, do you remember the account in the Bible of David's behavior when his first child with Bathsheba took deathly ill—"

"King David?"

"Old Testament—"

"Yes." Sam nodded.

"Well, Pastor might recall—" Chief Outlaw took a big bite of his greasy cheeseburger. "But I sure don't. So, fill me in."

"Well, the Bible says that King David prayed in sackcloth and ashes, begging the Lord to spare his child's life—"

"Yes." Pastor Jamie nodded. "It was his first child after he had sinned so horribly with Bathsheba; I do recall—"

"But when the child died," Sam continued, "the servants of King David were astonished. Having heard the bad news, David got up; washed himself; changed his clothes; and began to worship and praise the Lord—"

"Really!" Chief Outlaw said as he drowned his fries in ketchup. "That must've been really tough—"

"Yes, and when his servants asked him how…why?" Sam's eyes welled up with hot tears. "David said while the child was alive, he'd had the privilege of asking the Lord to spare its life—"

"But when the child died," Pastor Jamie said, taking up the story before Sam's tears could fall, "David had to accept God's will in the matter—"

"I bet that was hard—" the chief said, wiping the mustard off his chin with a napkin.

114

"Sure, it was hard...so very hard." Sam blinked back his tears. "But now...it's my turn. I prayed...we all prayed...that Samantha would be healed, live, and not die. So, now, in equal measure, I have to accept our Father's answer to our prayers. I have to accept His will in the matter...just like David did—"

"Man, I hear you—"

"Last night, the Lord showed me that it's time to let Samantha go...so I must let her go." Sam grimaced. "It's His call...not mine. It's His will...not mine. She's His child...not mine. And for me not to accept His will in the matter would be an affront to Samantha's life, to her steadfast faith...and to her precious memory," Sam said as he wrestled with his emotions. "But more than that, it would be impossible for me to go on if I don't trust the Lord...in everything. And, with His help, I must go on—"

"I hear you, my brother." Chief Outlaw's strong, dark face crumbled with compassion. "And I do...I understand—"

"Yes, Sam, no love can be greater than our love for the Lord." Pastor Jamie nodded.

"Because when it's all said and done," Sam said, "we are all born into this mean world to get to know Jesus; to get saved; and to go back home to live with Him. And everything else we do in this life is superfluous to this indisputable truth. And I'm thrilled that Samantha knew that, too." Sam drew in a long, deep breath and slowly released it. "And that's what I'll miss most...our oneness...our agreement in all things important—" While Sam's heart ached, his jawline set in firm resolve. And from that point on, he and his steadfast brothers shared their meal in silence.

CHAPTER 20

"Nurse Greene…Joy…I realize you've been through an awful lot…finding Samantha like you did," Sam said quietly. "But I…I wanted to take a moment to extend to you my sincerest thanks…on behalf of Samantha and myself…for all that you did to keep my wife safe and comfortable during your stay with us—"

"Oh, Sam, I'm so very sorry for your loss. But as you well know, it has been my privilege and pleasure to spend this time with you," Joy said, fixing her picture-perfect face accordingly—no face mask required. Her hair and makeup were flawless, and her pretty-in-pink, form-fitting dress tickled the tops of her knees to show-off her shapely calves." Oh, and by the way, Sam," Joy said, fluttering her lengthy lashes, "have you already made the funeral arrangements?"

"Yes, I have," Sam said. "Pastor Jamie and Chief Outlaw spent the day with me, helping me through the ordeal—"

"Oh, that was very nice." Joy glowed. "Pastor Jamie is such a dream…and his little family. In fact, our whole church family is just a jewel—"

"And it's been a distinct pleasure to get to know you as a church member and a nurse, Joy, but we all understand that you have to move on now. But rest assured, you can expect to receive my very highest commendation—"

"Oh, no, Sam!" Joy's mouth snapped shut. "I'm in no hurry to leave. In fact, I was planning to stay here for the funeral in honor of Samantha…and to help you through this very difficult time—"

"That's very kind of you, Joy…very kind, but—"

"And I'm willing to stay over…after the funeral…and finish up the Soup Kitchen project—"

"I'm sure that won't be necessary. I'm sure you need to move on to your next assignment…your next patient—"

"Usually, that would be the case, but I'm by no means a quitter." Joy rallied. "Pastor Jamie is very pleased with my work with the Food Pantry and on the Soup Kitchen project. And besides, Sam—" Joy whined, pursing her pretty, pink lips into a seductive pout. "I always like to finish what I've started—"

"Yes, Joy, Pastor Jamie has been singing your praises—"

"Oh, really?" Joy's smile sparkled, hearing that her plan was right on target. She'd been counting on the unsuspecting pastor to secure her place in Sam's heart. "Well, that's real sweet of him—"

"And as I understand it, Joy, you already have all the companies lined up to complete the renovation plans. Now, it's just a matter of final execution and punch-list items—"

"But Sam—" Joy's voice dropped to a plea. "What if…what if you should need me—"

"Well, to tell the truth, I'm terribly busy today," Sam said smoothly, although her obvious attempt at a come-on wasn't lost on him. He felt she was trying to force him to see her as a woman and not a nurse, and he wasn't prepared to deal with it. "So, I really don't have time to argue the point with you right now; but I'm quite sure if you speak with Pastor Jamie, he'll assign someone else to tie-up the final loose ends on the project…after you're gone—"

"But—"

"Sorry, Joy, gotta run." Sam bounded quickly for the exit and nearly collided into Mrs. Barnes who had stationed herself like a listening post in the doorway. "Oh! Please excuse me," he said, "I didn't see you standing there—"

"You're excused, Mr. Sterling; I'm sure," Mrs. Barnes said through clenched jaws. *But you ain't, Joy Greene…you fast-moving huzzy, you. I thought you were up to no good all along, and now you've proved me right. And I've gotta get your fast tail up outta here…and right away!*

"Oh, hi, there, Mrs. Barnes," Joy said sweetly.

"Hi, yo'self, Nurse Greene—" Mrs. Barnes twirled her eyes in Joy's general direction and swung out of the room to find the nearest telephone. She tiptoed to the elevator to avoid her squeaky shoes from giving her away, and she descended to the study to make her call. She was hoping to find complete privacy there. "Hello, is this Hope...Hope Greene?" Mrs. Barnes whispered into the receiver.

"Yes, it is. Who's this?"

"Well, I thought...after our good time together down here in the country...you'd remember my voice," Mrs. Barnes said, softening her tone to a smile.

"Yes, you do sound familiar," Hope said, "but I just can't seem to place—"

"You gave me your number...said I could call you any time. But I won't keep you in suspense. This is me...Lily...Lily Barnes...the Sterling's housekeeper down here in Sandywood—"

"Oh, that's right! It is you." Hope chuckled. "And how could I possibly forget the best cook in all of Georgia! How are you?"

"I'm doing just fine," Mrs. Barnes said softly, "but we're having a bit of trouble down here—"

"Trouble?" Hope frowned. "What sort of trouble?"

"I don't know if your cousin, Joy, told you...but Mrs. Sterling passed away—"

"Oh, no!" Hope groaned. "How's Mr. Sterling...Sam?"

"Mr. Sterling is holding his own, but he's terribly upset as you can imagine. His wife was his life. Her passing has ripped his heart out—"

"Yes, I can imagine," Hope groaned. "When I had that delightful time at his dining table that one night, all he could talk about was his beloved Samantha."

"Yes, honey, she was the love of his life." Mrs. Barnes paused poignantly. "You mean to tell me Joy didn't call and tell you 'bout her passing?"

"No, ma'am, I haven't heard from Joy since I left your house—"

"Well, do Jesus—"

"Has Joy gone back to Atlanta?"

"No…and that's kinda why I'm calling—"

"Oh?"

"The funeral service is planned for this weekend…and after the services, it would be nice if Nurse Greene would just go on back home—"

"Yes, ma'am—"

"But…I overheard her telling Mr. Sterling that she wanted to stick around here…in case he might need her—"

"Why would he need her?"

"'Xactly my point!" Mrs. Barnes huffed. "There ain't no reason for her to stick around here after the service is over. Everything will get back to normal a whole lot quicker when she's gone home. Mr. Sterling don't need no constant reminders about his wife's illness or her death…and he sho' don't need no help from the likes o' Joy! I'll be here to take care of him like always."

"Oh, I see," Hope said, remembering Joy's chilly predictions and her unholy designs on Sam Sterling's life.

"So…I was wondering, Hope…if you've got the time…can you perhaps come on back down here for the funeral…and help your cousin pack up her things and go on back home after it's over with." Mrs. Barnes lowered her voice. "And you don't even have to let on to Joy you're coming. I'm inviting you myself—"

"I think I understand, Mrs. Barnes, more than you know," Hope said. "It'll take a little doing because I have to find someone to look after my parents…they're rather poorly, you know. But, yes, ma'am; text me the information; and I'll make the arrangements to get there for the funeral—"

"And escort your cousin on back home afterwards?"

120

"Yes, ma'am. I'll make sure that Joy gets back home after the services; or maybe, I can talk her into coming back home to Kansas City with me for a visit—"

"There you go! After all she's been through, it may be good for her to be with her own people for a while," Mrs. Barnes said. "And you don't surprise me none. From the first time I laid eyes on you, Hope, I knew you had good, hard, common sense. And I knew you were the kind o' church sister I could count on in a pinch. Be blessed on your journey; and in the meantime, keep praying for Mr. Sterling. Sam's gonna need all the prayers he can get."

"Yes, ma'am, my prayers and condolences are with Sam…and with you, also. God bless you all! See you soon!"

CHAPTER 21

The homegoing service for Samantha Sterling would've been to her liking. From beginning to end, it was a celebration of the tender love, grace, and mercy of Jesus Christ. From the first note of the first praise song, Sandywood Bible Fellowship was filled with jubilation and gratitude for a life well lived. Pastor Jamie's eulogy was short and poignant; and at its conclusion, the invitation to accept Jesus Christ as Saviour and Lord was joyfully extended to the entire congregation. And beyond every expectation, one young man—who had grown up receiving many of his weekly meals with his mother and siblings in the church's Soup Kitchen—came forward to give his life to Christ. It was all the validation Samantha's life and service to her family, church, and community required.

Equally, there was no pageantry at the graveside—no doves or balloons were released, no verbose words were shared. There was only a simple prayer of benediction offered by Pastor Jamie. As they exited, no more tears were shed. All that remained was the fragrance of a beautiful life and the scent of the long-stemmed yellow roses—Samantha's favorite—which had been kindly provided to each of the attendees to place at her gravesite as they departed, including Hope Greene.

Hope did, in fact, make the funeral, much to her cousin, Joy's, dismay. Given the Covid protocols, seating had been limited at the church, but every seat had been taken. Hand in hand, Sam and Mrs. Barnes shared the family pew up front, while Hope sat alongside Joy near the back of the church. While sitting there, even in that sacred space, Hope couldn't help being distracted. The conversation she'd had with Joy upon her arrival was still making a vicious loop inside her skull.

****

"Hope, who asked you to come here?!?" Joy had demanded when they were finally alone in the guestroom that Mrs. Barnes had prepared. "How did you know—"

"Mrs. Barnes called to invite me, Joy. She thought you might need the support...and my help getting back home—"

"Help? Why would I need your help?!?" Joy steamed. "I'll leave here only when I'm good and ready and not before. And I don't give a rat's toenail about what Mrs. Barnes wants—"

"But, Joy, these people are hurting, and they need to get back to some semblance of a normal routine. Certainly, you can understand that—"

"So, it was Mrs. Barnes who put you up to this? Humph! Sounds like something she'd do—"

"Maybe. But, Joy, it is true—"

"True? How do you know what's true? Sam needs me—"

"Did he say he needed you—"

"Not in so many words, but—"

"But Joy...I do need you. I need your help—"

"You? Need my help—"

"Yes, Joy. I've had doctors and nurses coming and going in the care of mom and dad for years. I've tried to do all the research, but I need your expert opinion...about their condition and their continued care. I've been doing this alone for a long time; but, now, I really do need your help. And I'm sure your favorite...and only...uncle and aunt would love to see you again. They ask about you all the time—"

"Oh, Hope, I don't know—"

"But, Joy, you probably need a break. You've been at this for a while, and I know how close you were to Mrs. Sterling...and Mr. Sterling...and you probably just need some downtime...some time to step away. You know...like a vacation—"

"Vacation?"

"Well, I know Kansas City is not bright lights and tinsel, but it is your home. And it might do you good to get back to your roots for a while…you know…recharge, reenergize…and refocus—"

"Well, Hope, if you put it that way…I guess it wouldn't hurt me to spend a few weeks in Kansas City. It'll be good to see Aunt Faith and Uncle James again—"

"Right! And I'll show you the town. You've never even seen my business. And Kansas City has really grown-up since you've been away."

"So, when do you want to leave?"

"The day after the funeral—"

"So soon? But—"

"But, Joy, if there's anything for you here…I mean…if there's really anything you're leaving behind…if it's truly yours…certainly, it'll keep."

"Oh, I guess you're right." Joy fluttered like a wounded bird. "I probably do need a breather…time to clear my head. Besides, there's nothing that can stop me from coming back here whenever I choose! There's the church…and Sam. And Mrs. Barnes certainly can't keep me away—"

"You're right; I'm sure. So, come on. Get ready. Let's go home."

****

When everyone returned to the Sterling residence from the gravesite, Joy ran upstairs to pack while Hope went into the kitchen to help Mrs. Barnes prepare the repast for the mourners who'd gather to pay their respects. When Sam Sterling came in from the garage and saw Hope standing there, he pulled her aside.

"Hi, Hope," Sam said, "it's so good to see you again. I'm sorry we haven't had much time to talk—"

"I perfectly understand." Hope smiled. "I'm sure you've had a lot on your mind, Mr. Sterling, but the service was simply perfect—"

"No. Call me, Sam. And I'm very glad to hear you say that." His handsome mouth curled into a near smile. "I'm sure Samantha was pleased."

"I'm sure."

"Did Joy tell you about the funeral?"

"No…Mrs. Barnes—"

"Mrs. Barnes?"

"Yes, we exchanged contact info the last time I was here." Hope bit her lip. "And she thought that Joy might need some help…getting home—"

"Oh, I see—"

"And I think I've convinced her to come back to Kansas City with me." The dimple in Hope's left cheek sparkled like star lights, and Sam took special note. The baby fat that had plagued her as a child had long since fashioned itself into strong, attractive curves. "She hasn't been home in such a long time."

"Good news!" Sam said as his eyes drank in her beauty. "And I'm sure Joy's grateful for your support."

"So, then, Joy and I are preparing to get out of your hair." Hope giggled. "She's upstairs packing as we speak—"

"I do appreciate everything Joy did for my wife…but, now, her assignment is complete."

"Yes, and we'll be leaving tomorrow—"

"You're leaving? So soon?" Sam's eyes sparked. "Well, I'm just very glad you came, Hope. It's been so good to see you again. Your presence here gave me…the kind of balance I needed…old friends and new—"

"Me…but you hardly know me—"

"Oh, I know you," Sam retorted. "That one evening you shared dinner with us…hearing you talk about your childhood…*the twin cousins*…I learned a lot about you. And I could sense that Joy has one view of things, and you've been sheltering her from yours—"

"But how could you know—"

"Trust me; I know from experience. There're at least two sides to every family story." Sam gave her a knowing smile. "But throughout the evening, there was something about your patience and kindness toward Joy and her rose-colored glasses that brought me enormous peace."

"Really?"

"Could it be that we share...the same sense of loss...a lost love, maybe." Sam raised his brows with intense interest. "You'll have to tell me your story someday. I'm very interested to know—"

"But I'm sure Joy has been a great source of comfort to you as well—"

"In her own way...but as you know, Joy tends to...flutter." Sam shrugged. "Me...I like solid, praying women on my side—"

"But how do you know—"

"Trust me." Sam's eyes swept over Hope, from head to toe and back again. "I know," he said in a near whisper. He'd never expected to see her again; but, now, he was grateful for another chance. "I see you, Hope—"

"Oh-h, my—" Hope's cheeks flamed. In just those few words, Sam had managed to bypass her feelings of impotence and strike a fresh, new chord of excitement in her soul.

"Listen, Hope," Sam said quietly, "I've got a pretty big project that'll bring me to K.C. on business in the months to come, and I was wondering if I could take you out to dinner...or something...just sit and talk...and, maybe, we can take the time to explore our shared experiences—"

"Well...I don't know." Hope said, diverting her gaze from his intense, handsome eyes. "But I guess that would be alright. It would be good to see a familiar face and to know you're okay...and to find out how Mrs. Barnes is doing. Just keep me posted on your plans. I'll see what I can do to make myself available—"

"Perfect. I couldn't ask for more." Sam reached for Hope's hand and squeezed it gently. "Take good care of yourself, Hope—"

"You, too, Sam. You, too—"

CHAPTER 22

"Well, Hope, Uncle James and Aunt Faith appear to be holding their own, all things considered," Joy said clinically as they exited the family home on 71st Street in Kansas City, Missouri. "Their in-home caregivers seem to be on the ball, and I can see you've invested a lot of time and money to take good care of your parents."

"Thanks, Joy—"

"But it does appear they may be on too much medication—"

"Oh, do you think so?"

"Yes, that's the problem with doctors these days." Joy fluttered angrily. "They tend to shop their elderly patients around to all their colleagues, especially the ones with good insurance. And some of our seniors end up with more medications than they really need, and some of these drugs are actually contraindicated for each other."

"So, what can we do?"

"Well, I'll spend the next several weeks with you, taking Uncle James and Aunt Faith to their various doctor's appointments. And while we're there, I'll question the dosages and recommend that the doctors discontinue some of the meds."

"Thanks, Joy. I knew you'd know exactly what to do—"

"Well, don't get too excited, Hope. Changing their meds may not improve their prognosis or increase their longevity...but it just might make them feel better and more alert while they're here."

"And that's all I can ask—"

"But, in the meantime, Hope...their skin does appear to be a bit sallow." Joy pursed her pretty lips into a critical smirk. "And vitamin D is very important to their continued wellbeing. The pills help, of course, but the direct source is always better. So, in my professional opinion, I'd say they both could do with a bit more sunshine each day. They've been sitting around indoors far too long—"

"Okay," Hope said cheerfully. "Then I tell you what let's do. I'll arrange for the medical van to load them up with their wheelchairs and take them over to Swope Park tomorrow afternoon; and, then, we can meet them over there and wheel them around to your heart's content—"

"Um-hmm—" Joy pouted her perfect lips. "Sounds like *real* big fun—"

"Oh, Joy, you're so funny." Hope giggled. "But right now, I'm taking you for a ride. There's something I'd like for you to see. And, afterwards, I'll take you by Great's Barbecue, and you can get your grub on—"

"Great's! Yum! I love that place. Are they in the same location over there on Prospect?"

"Well, they've got a few new locations since you've been gone; but, sure, I'll take you to the one in the 'hood."

"Gurrl, I am so ready. Let's go!" Joy giggled as she folded her long, lean body into Hope's two-seater Audi with the drop top. And since summer was grudgingly giving way to fall, the weather was still unseasonably warm in Kansas City.

"And maybe Sunday, we can go to the morning service at our home church," Hope offered. "I know everybody at Greater Harvest would be thrilled to see you. They ask about you all the time."

"Hmm—" Joy reseated her custom-designed sunglasses and took in the sights, both old and new. "Nope…on that one, I'll have to take a hard pass. I don't even want to do a drive-by—"

"But what've you got against the church, Joy?"

"Nothing. Nothing at all. But that's your scene, not mine." She smoothed down her long, silky hair that was flowing freely in the breeze. "It really never was."

"Well, okay." Hope relented.

On their way uptown, Hope waded her car through a crowded parking lot and pulled into a spot marked, *Reserved*, at the front entrance.

"Why're we stopping here?" Joy puzzled as her eyes fell on the impressive, red-brick building that was branded with bold, beautiful signage. "And exactly who's parking space are you high jacking?"

"High jacking?" Hope chuckled. "Joy, this is my parking spot, and this is my building. This is *Hope Enterprises*...my business—"

"Your business?" Joy gaped. She was duly impressed by the size and grandeur of the site, and she was struggling to keep her surprise and admiration in check. "But...you told me you owned a little hair salon—"

"Well, that's how it started, Joy. But you've been gone a minute; and over the years, we've grown into this current location—"

"But this...this is beautiful, Hope! This building is...outrageous. The size...the colors...the branding...it's all so...tres chic!"

"Well, we try to please." Hope giggled happily. "C'mon, let's go inside—"

"But which side?" Joy stood back and took it all in. "As I see it, they're at least three entrances to this behemoth. There's one labeled, *Beauty*...I imagine that's hair, nails, and such. And there's also one labeled, *Body*...I imagine that's every spa delight. And there's one labeled, *Bounty*...and I'd venture a guess that's some sort of fancy juice bar, huh?"

"Well, not quite." Hope smiled. "We offer only a Mediterranean-styled menu with organic veggies, smoothies, waters...but no carbs, fats, or sugars—"

"Well, this...this is not a hair salon...this is more of a...lifestyle emporium." Joy's mouth gaped against her wishes. "Look at you, Hope. You've got beauty, body, and healthy eating all on lockdown. You've turned this into a...self-care paradise," Joy spouted, in equal measures amazement and envy. "You must gross well over a million dollars a year in this place—"

"Well...not quite." Hope flashed her a wink. "We're growing the business right now...but soon—"

"And I'm quite sure you've had lots of help pulling this off." Joy returned her wink. "So, who is your silent partner…your benefactor, hmm—"

"No benefactor," Hope said firmly as she guided Joy through the door labeled, *Beauty*. "But, yes, I do have a great team. We actually built this in stages, and then we tied it all together as a seamless unit under one roof. Let's step inside; shall we?"

Once inside, Joy did her best not to stare at the 50 or so work stations buzzing with uniformed stylists and smiling clients. "Hope, it looks like the United Nations up in here," Joy quipped. "You've got every race and nationality represented in this place."

"That's because we offer everything from perms to locs; facials to botox; nails to pedicures…and everything in between—"

"Oh, I can see that," Joy admitted. Plus, she couldn't overlook the fact that Hope—her twin cousin—had floor-to-ceiling posters scattered throughout the space, which bore her life-sized image and advertised her own, personalized line of fragrances and make-up— "Hope's Delight." *Say what!?!*

After a quick look-around, Hope led Joy through a set of sliding glass doors to the space aptly labeled, *Body*. It was an expansive spa area that provided every imaginable treat—from an Olympic-sized swimming pool; to a menu of personalized massages; and a fleet of on-staff trainers who offered instruction on the full gamut of exercise equipment. There were also specialized classes available in every discipline from martial arts to yoga.

On their way through the corridor, Joy had spotted a number of framed plaques on the trophy wall. So, she stepped back inside to take a closer look. "Kansas City Chamber of Commerce, Board of Directors…Hope Greene…hmm. Women's Business Council of Missouri…President, Hope Greene…hmm. Now, Hope, isn't this a national organization?"

"Yes, Joy, it is—"

"And you're the president of the entire Missouri Chapter?"

"Yes, Joy, I am."

"I guess you'd say that's quite an accomplishment, huh?"

"Well, I never really thought about it." Hope shrugged. "I just enjoy seeing women reach their full potential—"

"And I guess with all this," Joy said, swinging her arms around the full expanse of Hope's business enterprise, "you imagine you've reached your full potential, too, huh?"

"I didn't say that, Joy," Hope said almost shamefacedly."

"Well, I should say not!" Joy huffed. "You left your *full* potential behind when you walked out on me at Fisk! Yes, you could've been a doctor, Hope, but you settled for this!"

"Joy—"

"And why didn't you mention all of this to Sam? Tell him about your burgeoning business, huh? At least he would've seen my family has chops, too?"

"But what I do for a living never came up in the conversation—"

"No, it didn't...it never would...'cause you always try to be so modest. But being modest will get you late, Hope!"

"Joy—"

"No, you've gotta put yourself out there these days, or you'll get left behind. In today's culture, you've gotta self-promote, or you'll get stuck eating other people's dust while they beat you to the finish line—"

"And just what is the finish line?" Hope sparked.

"Having it all! What else?" Joy ticked off the finer points of her argument on her pretty fingers. "Recognition. Wealth. Notoriety. Fame. Powerful Family Connections...and to get it by any means necessary!"

"Joy, that sounds a li'l cut-throat, even coming from you—"

"And I can see you still haven't learned the lesson!" Joy stabbed at the plaques that honored Hope's commitment and influence in her community. "I can see you're still concerned for the other guy. Well,

133

the *other* guy is not concerned for you. You've gotta be concerned for you!"

"Joy—"

"I'd only get mixed-up with this bunch of yahoos," she shrieked, poking a wicked thumb at Hope's plaques, "if there was something in it for me!"

"Joy, we get lifted by lifting others—"

"Phooey! We get lifted by lifting ourselves!"

"But, Joy, this...this is my community...your community...our home—"

"But at least, now, I can see why you've been able to afford to take such special care of Uncle James and Aunt Faith—"

"That's my responsibility...my duty...my pleasure—"

"And why you were able to fly to Samantha's funeral on such short notice." Joy's hands flapped in agitation. "Yeah, but why did you come to the woman's funeral? Who asked you to come? Sam is my business, not yours!"

"Joy, I came...I came for you—" Hope lowered her voice in an attempt to get Joy to follow suit. She was making every effort to regain her composure and to preserve the sanctity of space for her clients who could undoubtedly hear their angry voices bouncing off the sliding glass doors. "Mrs. Barnes knew you were so invested in Mrs. Sterling's welfare that you might need...family support...in backing away. I came because I thought you needed me—"

"Needed you? Ha!" Joy blasted. "I don't need you! I don't need anybody! I've got my own plans—"

"I know. You told me. But, Joy, how do you know if Sam's even interested—"

"I've seen the look of love in Sam's eyes—"

"Yeah! Love for his wife...not for you—"

"But I can change that!" Joy paced tight loops in the corridor like a caged cat. "He's a man; isn't he? And men do what smart women like me tell 'em to do—"

"Joy, Sam is certainly a fine man, but he may not be ready yet…maybe, it's just too soon—"

"Don't you worry, Hope." Joy steamed. "I'm getting back with Sam. I'm sure he misses me. But if he doesn't, I'm very sure Pastor Jamie will find me to be indispensable when they try to access the church's contracts with those vendors for the Soup Kitchen. I made sure of it…only my password works—"

"Joy, how could you—"

"Hope, I've got my own life to lead." Joy's tiny nostrils flared. "And I don't need your sanctimonious clap-trap, especially since you're the one who punked out on me in Nashville. I became the top nurse. You were supposed to be the brilliant doctor. Remember?"

"But, Joy, I couldn't stay…there're some things you just don't know…about Uncle Jude—"

"Uncle Jude!?! Uncle Jude wasn't your problem. You're your problem!" Joy stormed. "You're always taking the easy way out. Well, I didn't! I stuck to my guns; and, now, I deserve the fruits of my labor. I've been tending to sick patients and putting up with their families and their whining long enough. I deserve my prize, and Sam Sterling is it!"

"Joy! You've always wanted everything your own way and on your own terms—"

"And I wanted the same for you, too, Hope…for us. We had a master plan, but you were too chicken-hearted to stick with it!" Joy shrilled. "And you forced me to have to go about it my own way. So, whatever I am today…whatever I've become…whatever I've done …well, it is all your fault!"

"Joy, what're you saying—"

"It doesn't matter! Nothing matters!" Joy brushed Hope aside. "All I know is Sam Sterling is a man of action; and when I'm by his side, we'll be the power couple of the decade. The world will be our oyster and Georgia our footstool!"

"So, what you're saying is you want to use Sam for your own ends—"

"You can call it what you will, but know this…Sam Sterling is mine!"

"But what if this grandiose scheme of yours doesn't work—"

"Oh, it'll work." Joy sneered. "I've already set it in motion—"

"Joy—"

"Make no mistake, Hope! I'm gonna get what's mine! I just need you…all of you…to stay outta my way!" Joy straight-armed Hope and raced for the exit amid the wide-eyed stares of startled clients who, heretofore, had never experienced negative energy in the house that Hope built. "And you can just carry your own sick folk to the doctor!" Joy kicked open the door. "I'm out!"

Trailing behind her to the exit, Hope clasped her hands together at her heart's center into a prayer pose. And with a sincere bow and an apologetic smile, she signaled for her clients to get back to the serious business of relaxing and enjoying themselves. "Namaste!"

CHAPTER 23

"Well, Sam, thanks for inviting me over," Chief Rufus Outlaw said while taking a seat in his home office, big hat in hand. "I really need to talk to you—"

"Of course, Chief." Sam nodded and offered him a genuine smile from behind his see-through, acrylic desk. It served as an expression of his commitment to total transparency—not only for his successful company, but in his own personal life as well. "So, how can I help you this fine morning?"

"Well, I guess you've read the news? About how our previous coroner, Buster Clayton, went and got himself indicted for fraud and dereliction of duty."

"Yes, Chief, I saw the article, and it's a sad state of affairs when our public officials abandon their integrity—"

"Yeah, Sam, but that ain't even the half of it." The chief fumed. "What the papers didn't tell you," he said, keeping a sharp eye on the closed door, "and what I'm about to tell you…well, it can't ever leave this room—"

"Okay, Rufus, I understand—"

"You see; it's pretty certain that they'll also be indicting Buster Clayton as a co-conspirator in that murder case involving that bad man…Lex Lee—"

"Lex Lee? Wasn't he recently acquitted for murdering his wife?"

"Yup! It created quite a stir; all over the national news, too. But now it seems that our disgraced coroner, Buster Clayton, tampered with some o' the crucial forensic evidence in that case, which just might blow-back on him, big time."

"Is that a fact?"

"Like I told you before; I don't know if Buster was incompetent or just plain stupid, but his secret shenanigans got found out pretty quick-like by our new coroner—"

"I understand the new man is Dr. Franklin Forester—"

"Yes, indeedy, and he comes to us from Miami with impeccable credentials and a squeaky-clean record. But he's kinda getting up in age, you know; and him and his wife, well, they just wanted to move to a more seasonal climate with less traffic and such—"

"That's understandable—"

"But, Sam, it didn't take the man long to figure out there was a dead monkey on the line somewhere with our previous coroner and his findings. And a few days after coming on board, Doc Franklin found irrefutable proof that Buster Clayton had tampered with evidence in the Lex Lee murder case; and his blasted treachery has let a guilty man off, scot-free—"

"So, how was Franklin Forester able to figure it out so quickly?"

"It was that stupid, Buster Clayton! He left a computer trail and a paper trail a mile wide," the chief said. "And there's a money trail, too. I don't think he ever figured anybody would backtrack his work. He didn't even bother to destroy the evidence that proved that Lex Lee killed his wife; or maybe, just maybe, he was tryna keep it in his back pocket to shake him down later. I don't know. But as it turned out, Doc Franklin happened to open up some of the recent back cases just so he could see his way clear going forward—"

"And that's when he uncovered the conspiracy, huh?"

"Yup, and after he was holding the smoking gun, so to speak, the District Attorney's Office had their investigators look into Buster's bank accounts and spending patterns—"

"And they could tell that he took a bribe?"

"Did he? Yes, he did!" Chief Outlaw whooped. "But it wasn't in the form o' no money—"

"No?"

"No! That joker was tryna be slick. He had Lex Lee buy him a yacht and a real high-dollar condo in South Florida; and later on, he transferred it into his own name. But there's no doubt in anybody's mind that it was the payoff for tampering with the evidence in that murder case—"

"Guess he was setting himself up for a real nice retirement—"

"Fool! Like we wouldn't be able to track all o' that down." Chief Outlaw sneered. "Like I said, Sam, I really don't think the man is too bright. But anyhoo, he's in deep kamancheh, now, and there's no way out for him. They may not be able to get Lex Lee on the murder charge again…double jeopardy and all that kind o' jazz…but they'll certainly nail him on bribery, fraud, conspiracy, embezzlement, and anything else they can trump-up against him. The district attorney is pretty steamed about getting hoodwinked. And by the time they get done racking-up all o' them charges and tying up all o' his assets, Lex Lee's gonna wish he had o' gone down for murder—"

"But what was his motive—"

"Seems Lex Lee killed his wife 'cause she'd caught him red-handed embezzling from her big trust fund, and she was about to blow the whistle on him to her daddy who's a mighty powerful man in this state. And, now, Buster Clayton gets to wear the dunce cap of the year 'cause he's gonna find himself in a jail cell right next to that murderer—"

"And that's all very interesting, Chief…in a sad sort o' way…but I know you didn't come all this way to tell me that—"

"No, Sam, I've gotta shoot you straight." Chief Outlaw gripped onto his big hat. "But you're not gonna like it. Naw…you're not gonna like it one, li'l bit—"

"Just say it, Rufus. You know you can tell me anything, and it'll stay right here in this room. You have my word—"

"That's not the problem, Sam." Rufus Outlaw's voice sank to a deep whisper. "I've got…a BIG ask for you—"

"What is it, Rufus? What's all the suspense?"

"Well, you see, Sam...because our former coroner was showed up to be a crook like he was...well, it's kinda put a cloud over the whole department...the whole justice system—"

"I don't understand—"

"Well, the defense attorneys in all of the cases we've prosecuted using Buster Clayton's findings are lining up to dispute his evidence in their cases, too. They're lining up to get the old cases overturned because all o' that scoundrel's work has now come under closer scrutiny—"

"Oh, I see—"

"And, Sam, if their claims hold up, it's gonna be like a firestorm burning through the whole courthouse. It'll cripple us from going forward for years. We've already got a terrible backlog on account of Buster being so blasted slow. And, now, if we're forced to wade through all o' his old cases, too, we'll never get our heads above water again. And then there'll be all the lawsuits against the county and the state claiming wrongful imprisonment and stuff like that. It could cripple us and make a mockery of the entire justice system—"

"So, what do you expect me to do about it, Rufus? Why're you here? How can I possibly help you get out of this mess—"

"But you can help, Sam! That's why I'm here—"

"But how?"

"Okay...well...the new coroner, Doc Franklin, has come up with a sure-fire solution. And I think it just might work—"

"I'm listening—"

"He...Doc Franklin, that is...he has developed a true random sampling of all o' Buster Clayton's old cases. Doc proposes that we...uhh...exhume the bodies in those cases...and just see if Buster Clayton made any other errors...by accident or on purpose. You see, that way, if the sample shows that he didn't tamper with evidence or negatively affect the outcome of any of his other autopsies, then maybe the defense attorneys, who are gathering like jackals around a fresh kill, won't have a leg to stand on. We'll be able to show that

Buster Clayton tampered with the evidence in just that one case involving Lex Lee…and then we'll be home free and clear, and things can get back to normal rather quickly."

"Makes sense." Sam nodded. "I see your point, Chief, but I still don't see what that has to do with me—"

"Well, the *B-part* of this whole thing is this, Sam. We've also got to prove that Buster Clayton was not in dereliction of his duties in all of his previous cases we examine. We've got to show…beyond a shadow of a doubt…that he was thorough and even-handed in the execution of his office in all of his other cases—"

"And—"

"And…Sam…uhhh…one of the cases that has popped-up in the random sample that Doc Franklin came up with…well…well, it's Samantha—"

"Chief, are you out yo' mind!?!" Sam leapt up from behind his desk. "My wife's been gone for less than a month…and you expect me to let you exhume her body…remove her from her final resting place…just because some lousy, crooked coroner went rogue?!?"

"Well…Sam…uhh…yeah…something like that—"

"No, Rufus, it is not something like that…it is absolutely that!" Sam shrilled. "And I'm not about to let you do it! No way!"

"But Sam, you have to—"

"No, I do not! Pick somebody else!"

"We can't. We need you, man," the chief pleaded. "This is a true random sample…it's like the lottery…it needs one-hundred-percent participation. The only way it works is if each and every number that was randomly selected…and each and every body that's associated with that number…is exhumed and re-examined by Dr. Franklin Forester." Chief Outlaw quickly raised both of his sweaty palms in complete surrender, allowing his big hat hit the floor. "I know, Sam! I know! It's a lousy deal! But it's a lousy deal for all the families, not just yours. But there's no other way. We need you, Sam. We need you to help us out o' this jam that could cost the taxpayers millions in bogus claims; not to mention, it could clog up the legal system for years!" Chief Outlaw made his impassioned plea while Sam Sterling slowly shook his head in disbelief. "Well, look at all the violent criminals that could be put back out on the streets on some trumped-up legalities. Look at all the ones that might not ever get to trial or be put away for their crimes due to some bogus, legal hangup. I know it's a BIG ask, Sam, but we need you, man! Your community needs you—"

"Enough!" Sam hammered his fist against his desk and braced himself up on it. "I hate this idea with a blazing passion...but I know Samantha had a love for justice through her work with the orphanage and the court system—" He stopped, steadied himself, and released a loud, deep sigh. "And I know she would be the first to say we need to help justice move forward...at any cost—"

"Thank you, Sam! Thank you—"

"No! Don't thank me. Don't you ever thank me for this, Rufus. This is detestable!" Sam flopped back into his chair, head in hands. "Thank Samantha...she's the only one who would've been selfless enough to agree to such a cruel and fool-hearted stunt—"

"I'll go now, Sam...and give you some space." Chief Outlaw retrieved his big hat and crushed it between sweaty palms. "But I'll be back soon with the papers for you to sign—"

"Oh, just come back and join us for dinner, Rufus," Sam said with a hung-down head. "I'll tell Mrs. Barnes to set an extra place. We eat promptly at 6 p.m."

CHAPTER 24

"Well, Sam, I invited you to my office today so we can have a li'l chat." Chief Outlaw reared back in his chair and tugged down on his 10-gallon hat.

"I gathered as much, Chief, and I came as soon as I could; even though I can't imagine what more you could possibly ask of me." Sam shrugged, still miffed from their previous encounter. "And I need to get back to my office as quickly as possible. I have a number of key meetings lined-up for this afternoon—"

"I figured you was plenty busy, Sam," Chief Outlaw drawled, understanding his reticence for having another face-to-face. "But this can be as long…or as short as you like—"

"Make sense, Rufus," Sam snapped. "I've got work to do—"

"Mr. Sterling," Chief Outlaw's voice took on an official tone as he was determined to maintain tight control of his meeting. "It is my duty to inform you of our new coroner's findings in your wife's recent exhumation." The chief thumbed deliberately through his notes. "Case No. EX-1012."

"Oh? Okay—" Sam said, settling into his seat.

"Seems like your wife's case has been one big comedy of errors—"

"How so?" Sam frowned.

"Not the *ha-ha* kind, Sam…more like the *oh-Lawd* kind—"

"What? What are you saying?"

"When Dr. Franklin Forester re-examined Samantha's body…he found some irregularities, some inconsistencies…and also something that's just down-right peculiar—"

"Oh? Some more mistakes made by the old coroner?"

"No-oo, nothing like that." The chief's eyes blazed. "He found chemo drugs in your wife's system, as you might imagine; but they were at such high levels and irregular concentrations that our new coroner went over her entire body with a fine-toothed comb—"

"And?"

"And Doc Franklin was able to locate a small wound...a small puncture wound...situated between the big toe on her left foot—"

"Puncture wound?"

"Yes, indeed. It appears that there had been an injection in that location...anti mortuum—"

"While she was still alive?"

"Yes, Sam. And there is no medical reason for Samantha to have been receiving injections in her foot, not during the entire course of her treatment. Doc Franklin double-checked that with Samantha's doctor," Chief Outlaw said, fingering through his notes, "a Dr. Wallace; am I right?"

"Right. Dr. Wallace was Samantha's doctor—"

"And Dr. Wallace agreed that a needle mark on Samantha's foot would be highly irregular and unwarranted—"

"So, what are you saying, Rufus?"

"We're saying that someone has injected a lethal dose of chemo drugs into Samantha's system...through her foot...which caused her premature death—"

"WHAT?!? Sam fell back into his chair—stricken. "WHO?!?"

"Think about it, Sam. Who else?"

"You mean...you think." Sam shook his head violently as he considered the possible suspects. "You think...Nurse Greene? You think...Joy Greene?!?"

"Who else? Who else would have the technical know-how? Who else had the access? Who else had the opportunity—"

"Joy?!? Killed...my wife?!?"

"That's not to say," Chief Outlaw added quickly, "that Samantha was not terminally ill. She was a very sick woman. In fact, according to our coroner, Samantha only had a few weeks to live…because the cancer had spread throughout all her vital organs—"

"Oh, no!" Sam gasped. "So, what you're telling me is that Nurse Greene…Joy…robbed me and my loving wife of our final precious moments together—"

"Face facts, Sam." Chief Outlaw's wide nostrils flared. "Besides you, there were only three people allowed to go near your wife…Dr. Wallace, Mrs. Barnes, and Nurse Greene. And based on what I understand, Dr. Wallace was never left alone with Samantha. Nurse Greene was always in attendance—"

"Or me—"

"Right! Besides, what would be his motive, anyhow? And a hot-shot between the toes is a straight-up crackhead move that our Mrs. Barnes would know nothing about—"

"Never!"

"So—"

"It was Joy!" Sam slumped into his chair, babbling like a broken man. "It's a fact. Nurse Joy Greene…killed…my wife. But why, Rufus…why?"

"Motive?" Chief Outlaw attempted to contain a vicious sneer that had been brewing in his gut for some time. "Sam, a young gold-digger like that don't need no motive; she only needs a plan! 'Cause from the first moment I laid eyes on her, I knew she had eyes for you. When she brushed Samantha's name aside on our very first meeting, I knew she was up to no good." The chief's left eyebrow twitched as it did under these circumstances, and he soothed it with his right index finger. "Her plan was always to take Samantha's place and to get next to you, my brother…she just speeded up the timetable—"

"But why?" Sam anguished. "Samantha was just starting to speak again. And Dr. Wallace was trying to get her strong enough to write again. I was so hopeful—"

"And, just maybe, it was that li'l ole fact right there that was Samantha's undoing—"

"What? Why?"

"Maybe, there was something Joy didn't want Samantha to tell you; ever think o' that?" Chief Outlaw gave him a knowing wink. "Your wife was a mighty smart cookie. And, maybe, she knew what Joy was up to. And, maybe, Joy didn't want her talking to you about it. Who knows what Joy was doing or saying to your wife when your back was turned?"

"If all this is true…and it must be…I shudder to think how that evil woman might've tortured my sweet, trusting Samantha while she was entrusted in her care," Sam said, bolting upright in his seat and taking on warrior eyes. "And my darling Samantha deserved better than that! Much better!"

"Oh, yes, she did!" Chief Outlaw agreed with a stiff nod. "We thought Nurse Greene was bringing *joy* to Sandywood. How could we have known she was bringing sadness and death?"

"Oh, Rufus—"

"Besides, who knows? That girl may have some…some kinda sociopathic or psychopathic tendencies…or some combination of the two—"

"Say what?"

"I've been reading up on that kinda stuff, you know…the kinda stuff that goes on in the mind of a nut-job—"

"Oh—"

"And all that's well and good," Chief Outlaw said, stripping off his big hat and getting down to serious business. "But now…now, Sam, it's our turn to do something about it—"

"But what can we do?" Sam agonized.

"We've got to lure Joy back down here to Sandywood so we can arrest her sorry tail—"

"But she has no reason to come back here, Rufus. After what she's done, why in the world would she come back here—"

"For you, Sam…you're still the prize—"

"I'm the what?!? The prize?!?

"Yes, man. Think about it! Joy wanted Samantha out o' the way. She wanted to take Samantha's place, and surely there can only be one reason why…you…and your great, big bank account!"

"Rufus, I never gave Joy any reason to think she'd ever have a ghost of a chance with me—"

"But, Sam, a selfish, greedy woman like her doesn't need your permission. She wants what she wants; and that's that. But, now, we've got to get her back down here so we can deal with it—"

"But wouldn't it be quicker to just dispatch law enforcement wherever she is and have them arrest her?"

"But if we happen to miss her, we're screwed." Chief Outlaw lamented. "If she even gets a hint that we're looking for her, we're screwed. Joy has a passport and connections all over the world through her nursing network. If law enforcement should fail to grab her up, she could get out o' our reach; out o' the country; and we'd never see her again—"

"So, what can we do?"

"Sam, I want you to make contact with her—"

"Me!"

"Yes, man, I want you to sweet talk her…tell her that you need to see her…need her to come to your house down here—"

"Are you out yo' mind, man? I can't talk to that woman! I can't stand THAT WOMAN! And if I ever see her again, I'll put my hands around her throat and—"

"Now-now, Sam, that's the wrong attitude," Chief Outlaw said, tongue in cheek, in an attempt to cool his own hot temper as well. "We've gotta be better than that. We've gotta be shrewd and level-headed about this thing. And you can-not…by any means…ever let on to Joy what you know. You can't let her get a whiff that we're on to her twisted game. Otherwise, we might lose her for good. And you don't want that; now, do you?"

"No!" Sam's hazel eyes blazed. "But if I ever see that woman again, I tell you...I will not be responsible for my actions—"

"Now, you've gotta calm yourself down, Mr. Sterling! And get yourself focused!" Chief Outlaw commanded. "This is very serious business, here, and it's too important to botch. You're the only one she'd come back to this neck of the woods for. She knows what she did, but she doesn't know we know...at least not yet." The chief made deliberate eye contact with Sam. "And she'd come back here for you...and only you. And we don't want her scampering out of the country with that passport of hers; now, do we? With her skills and connections, she could live anywhere in the world...even in those countries where we don't have an extradition treaty to haul her sorry behind back here to face this murder charge. And we don't want her to get away with this; now, do we, Mr. Sterling?"

"No!" Sam sobered. "We certainly do not want to lose her. She's got to pay for what she did to Samantha...to me...to us...denying us our final moments together—"

"And pay, she will!"

"So, what do you want me to do?"

"I want you to make contact with her...sweet talk her...tell her that you need her...need her to come back down here to your house 'cause...'cause you can't live without her...or whatever—"

"Don't you worry. I will put on the Academy-Award winning performance of a lifetime to get that woman back to Sandywood." Sam's voice hollowed. "But how will I ever find the words to tell Mrs. Barnes—"

"No! Oh, naw, Sam, you can't do that! You cannot, under any circumstances, let on to Mrs. Barnes. She loathes that woman...and always has...more than you do right now. If she knows the facts, her face will surely spill the beans; and we can't have that. So, I'm afraid...regardless of how loyal we know Mrs. Barnes to be...you've got to keep her in the dark about our li'l plan until we've sprung the trap on this cold-blooded killer...this Nurse *Joy* Greene—"

"Well, alright, Rufus, if you say so—"

"Yes, Sam. You go home right now and call that lying, li'l heifer! Let your words drip like honey. Lure Joy Greene back down here to Sandywood. And I promise you; it won't be too hard. She thinks she's so darn smart and irresistible. You just set the trap. And I guarantee you; we'll spring it." Chief Outlaw plumped his thick lips and rocked his head from side to side. "It's like my dear old mama used to say: 'You can catch more flies with honey than vinegar.'"

"Alright, Chief—" Sam's shoulders drooped heavily under the pain and the enormity of this unexpected revelation. "Whatever you say—"

"C'mon, now! Get yo'self together, man!" Chief Outlaw willed Sam back into action. "We're in a race for time, my brother! We've got a killer on the loose!"

CHAPTER 25

"Hel-lo," Joy said in her sexiest voice when she saw Sam Sterling's number pop-up on her phone.

"Hi. Is this Joy...Joy Greene—"

"Oh, Sam!" Joy giggled lusciously. "Of course, this is me. You dialed my number; didn't you?"

"Well, yes," Sam said, trying to choke back the angry bile rising up in his throat. "I was just unsure...if I'd dialed the right number."

"Well, of course, you did, silly," Joy said eagerly. "What's up? How've you been? It's so great to hear your voice—"

"Oh...I'm okay." Sam breathed into his anger. "And...how are you?"

"I'm just perfect." Joy giggled. "And even better now that I'm hearing from you."

"Well, it's good to hear your voice, too." Sam lied. "We all miss you...miss you down here in Sandywood."

"Yes, how is everybody?" Joy said glossily. "Mrs. Barnes...and Pastor Jamie? They miss me, too...hmm?"

"Yes, Joy, of course," Sam stammered. "We all...all of us...we miss you...very much."

"Well, that's good to hear." Joy pushed back her long hair with one hand and readjusted the phone closer to her ear with the other. "Because I miss all of you, too...desperately—"

"Well...I guess that's why I'm calling—"

"I thought you would've called before now, Sam—"

"Well, I would've, but—"

"Oh, Sam, I understand. It was your mourning period," Joy said sympathetically. "Well, I'm glad that's all over with now because it's so important to move on...after the inevitable has happened. There's nothing more we can do, so we must rally. Am I right?"

"Rally? Why, yes." Sam's throat gagged on every word. "Of course...you're right."

"See!" Joy cheered. "I knew you would see things my way—"

"And you did say before you left, Joy," Sam said quickly before he lost his nerve, "you said you might come back this way sometime soon...for a visit—"

"I did say that, and I meant it, Sam. That is...if I'm needed...or if I'm wanted——"

"Well, Pastor Jamie surely needs you." Sam eked out a chuckle. "Seems he's all thumbs over there since you left...especially with that Soup Kitchen project."

"So, Pastor Jamie's having a little trouble moving things forward without me, huh?" Joy smiled. She was thrilled to hear her scheme to bog things down was working swimmingly.

"Yes," Sam admitted. "He misses you, and your know-how for the project is invaluable—"

"And you, Sam, do you miss me?"

"Well...of course, I do, Joy," Sam tripped over his words. "Mrs. Barnes and I...well, we both miss you. You were the one bright spot in my home—"

"I'll just bet she does," Joy snipped. "But I'm very glad you miss me, Sam—"

"I do!" Sam said, framing the lie with all the energy he could muster. "Joy, I really, really do."

"Now, that is good to hear." Joy's voice smiled. "I really do like the sound of that, Sam—"

"So, I was just wondering," Sam said, trying not to sound too eager. "I was just wondering if you'd consider coming back down this way for a visit...real soon—"

"Well—"

"Joy, I know you're busy, and I wouldn't want to interrupt your business plans or anything like that; but when you're free...if you're ever free—"

"Oh, Sam, there's no need to sit up and beg." Joy's voice tinkled like the sound of wedding bells. "And if I'd known I meant so much to you, I would've been there before now—"

"Well, it would mean a lot to Pastor Jamie, too." Sam scrambled for just the right words. "It's like I said; he can't seem to make ends meet since you left—"

"No need to explain, Sam," Joy said dreamily. "It's enough to know you miss me, and you can't do without me. It's very flattering for a girl to feel indispensable, you know—"

"Oh...okay—"

"So, I'll take you off the hook." Joy giggled. "Because I know your courting skills are a bit rusty—"

"Oh, wow...thanks," Sam said, feigning gratitude and recalling Chief Outlaw's spot-on prediction that Joy would take the lead; her blind pride and her vain ego demanded it.

"So, I tell you what I'll do—"

"Okay—"

"I'll just move a few things around...and I can get there...let's say...early next week...let's make it Monday, in fact. How does that sound?"

"Oh, Joy, that'll be great!" Sam said, genuinely eager. "I can't wait to see you again...that is, we can't wait to see you again. And I'll be sure to let Pastor Jamie know he can expect you, too. It'll make his day!"

"Well, I'm just glad I can find the time," Joy said with an air of professionalism. "It's not always easy for me to move things around, but I am very much looking forward to seeing you, Sam...and, of course, the others as well."

"Thanks, Joy," Sam said earnestly. "You just don't know how much this means to me—"

"But I'm quite sure I'll find out." Joy's voice tinkled seductively. "And trust me; I'll be ready, too, Sam."

"I just bet you will." Sam's voice smiled sincerely for the first time in months. "And I'll be sitting on ready myself, Joy. You can believe that. I can hardly wait to see you!"

"And that's what I like to hear," Joy said with a satisfied giggle as she ended the call. "Bye-bye, for now.

"Oh…Mrs. Barnes?" Sam turned from his phone just in time to see her lurking ominously in his doorway.

"Mr. Sterling, did I just overhear you inviting that huzzy, Joy Greene, back into your home?" She steamed.

"Well, Mrs. Barnes," Sam said with fake indignation, "I don't think that's any of your business—"

"Not my business?" Mrs. Barnes sparked. "You sho' right about that! It ain't none o' my business!" She rocked one hand on her hip. "And I've tried to keep my mouth shut 'til now, but I just can't stand it! I can't stand seeing you make the worse mistake of your whole life by inviting that…that *creature* back down here," she said, nearly in tears.

"But Mrs. Barnes…Lily…you don't understand." Sam's woeful eyes plead. "And I don't have time to explain it all to you right now—"

"Ain't no need for no explanations!" Mrs. Barnes huffed. "You been like a son o' mine for all these years, Sam. And I know what you're doing ain't none o' my business. You're a full-growed man, and this right here is yo' house. But let me tell you *this* about *that*! If Joy Greene ever steps her foot back in this house…I'm out!" Mrs. Barnes stiffened her back; dried her eyes with the backs of her worn hands; and twirled for the exit. "And you can mark my words on that one, Mr. Sterling! You can mark my words!"

CHAPTER 26

"Well, hello, Mrs. Barnes," Joy said with a syrupy grin when the front door at 2200 Bird of Paradise Road swung open to welcome her back to Sandywood, Georgia. It was nearly seven months to the day of her first visit to her dream home. But unlike the first Monday, this time she was dressed to the nines. "You're looking quite well, Mrs. Barnes…for an elderly lady—"

"Hello, yo'self." Mrs. Barnes tugged on her salt-and-pepper wig. "What you doing back in these parts?"

"Oh? Didn't Sam tell you?" Joy swooped back her immaculate, dark curls and removed her custom sunglasses. "I'm Mr. Sterling's invited guest."

"Well, then, come on in." Mrs. Barnes unlocked the storm door with a flourish and permitted Joy to enter the foyer. "And excuse me," she said while reaching around her to retrieve her suitcase that was stationed beside the front door.

"Going somewhere, are we?" Joy said smugly. "Hmmm?"

"Yes, ma'am, Nurse Greene." Mrs. Barnes forced out the words through gritted teeth. "If you're coming in, I'm most definitely leaving out!"

"Tsk. Tsk." Joy giggled. "Now, don't be a sore loser; turn around is fair play. Just leave out gracefully…like I was forced to do when you called my cousin, Hope, to roust me up outta here." Joy rocked her head defiantly. "Do you remember that?!?"

"Yeah, I remember it, and I'm only sorry it didn't take," Mrs. Barnes said as she situated all of her luggage onto the front porch. "Mr. Sterling is in his office. Just make yo'self at home—"

"Don't you worry; I will." Joy took a twirl around the foyer like she was a returning conqueror. "That's exactly what I plan to do," she said as she slammed and locked the front door in Mrs. Barnes' face.

"Jo-y?"

"Oh, Sam…hi!" Joy's heart quickened when she turned to find him standing there. "It's Monday! I'm here!"

"And, so, you are." Sam gave her a half-smile. "And right on time, too, I see."

"Sam, you know I pride myself in punctuality." Joy stood erectly to give him a full view of her beauty. She was wearing a red, fitted knit dress with red-bottom stilettos to match and gold karat jewelry for a little added pop and shine.

"Yes, I do." Sam nodded approvingly. "And you look fantastic, Joy. Let's go down to the kitchen, and I'll fix you a little snack."

"Oh, Sam, I don't want anything to eat." Joy flipped back her hair. "Really—"

"But I do," Sam said, leading the way. "I've had a busy morning already."

"Oh, alright." Joy trailed him, a little disappointed at his semi-sweet greeting. She expected him to engulf her body in his arms, disarming her in desperate hugs and drowning her in flaming kisses.

"So, how was your drive down?" Sam asked as he pulled turkey and ham from the fridge.

"Uneventful."

"That's good."

"And what're you working on that's got you so distracted?" Joy said as she moved close enough for Sam to smell her classy perfume. "Hmm?"

"Oh…it's just another project," Sam said, reaching around her to secure a carving knife from the drawer.

"But, Sam, aren't you glad to see me?" Joy wrapped her arms around his waist in an attempted embrace.

"Well, of course, I am," Sam said while disentangling himself from her clutches. Her touch felt like an acid bath against his skin.

"I'm just not used to having a woman in the house…like you," he said. The carving knife was trembling in his right hand; but instead of turning it on Joy, he made slashing strokes into the ham.

"You mean one who looks as pretty as me…and feels as good as me?" Joy said, rebounding from his obvious rebuff.

"Sure. Right." Sam plunged the knife deep into the ham and quickly stepped away from it. "I don't know; maybe it's just too soon—"

"Too soon!" Joy gasped. "After all I've done for you…how can it possibly be too soon?"

"Done for me?" Sam leapt at the opening. "What exactly have you done for me, Joy?"

"Sam, don't you know?" Joy strutted around the kitchen like she owned the place. "I have been looking out for you from the very first moment I set foot into your lovely home—"

"Oh, really? How so?"

"I looked out for you. I protected you from the very start—"

"Protected me…from what?"

"From everything! Isn't it obvious?" Joy threw up her dainty hands in abject frustration. "From the seriousness of your wife's illness; from her rapid decline…and…and from all the ugly things she said against you—"

"My wife would never say anything against me—"

"You'd be surprised what sordid tales I've heard when people are deathly ill and in the throes of delirium—"

"Tales? What sordid tales?"

"You'd be surprised." Joy turned the screws deeply and slowly for maximum effect. "You'd just be surprised the things my patients have confided in me in the most loving of homes during my tenure as a hospice nurse—"

"What things?"

"Every family tree holds secrets, Sam." Joy smiled smugly. Her bogus insinuation had no basis in fact, but she was casting a broad net baited with a giant red herring.

"What!?! What did Samantha tell you?" Sam eyes flared wildly. *Surely, my wife didn't spill our family secret to this raving lunatic! No way!*

Bingo! Joy's eyes sparked with satisfaction. She'd been probing for a chink in Sam's armor, and it appeared she'd knifed him straight in his underbelly. "But I won't tell, Sam, if you won't tell—"

"What did Samantha tell you, Joy?"

"She said she hated you!" Joy lied for full effect, slinging the accusation squarely into Sam's face. "Your darling Samantha...your precious, Samantha...hated your guts! She always had! And she even hated the very sight of you toward the end. Couldn't you tell?"

"Lies! All lies!"

"She hated you, Sam...but I love you. Don't you see? I love you, Sam Sterling...more than you'll ever know!" Joy fluttered around the kitchen like a bird without a nest. "And I thought when she was gone...when she was out of our way...you would love me, too. Not that fragile kind of love that you had for poor, pitiful Samantha. No! Our love would be stronger, bolder, better...so much better!"

"Love!" Sam growled. "What love? I've never said anything to you about love—"

"But don't you see, Sam? She was just dead weight, and I had to protect you! Don't you know everything I did...everything I've ever done; I did for you...for us?"

"What did you do?" Sam bridled his rage to seize the moment.

"I didn't do anything! I didn't do anything wrong—"

"Liar!" Sam's face blazed with rage. "You killed her! You killed my wife!"

"I didn't! I didn't kill her!" Joy stepped back, frightened by the flame burning in Sam's hazel eyes. "The disease killed her...was killing her! I just helped her! I helped her get to a better place! Isn't that what you Jesus-freaks are always saying—"

"Murderer!" Sam lunged at Joy, grabbing her by the neck with both of his hot hands.

"No, Sam! No!" Chief Outlaw shouted into Sam's earwig and rushed from the next room to stave off his attack. "No! Don't do it!" the chief yelled as he ripped Sam's hands away from Joy's slender throat. "She's not worth it, man! She's not worth it! Let us handle it!"

"No! No! Take your filthy hands off me!" Joy screeched at Chief Outlaw. "Sam! Oh, Sam! I love you, Sam! Don't you see? I love you!"

"Joy Greene," Chief Outlaw pronounced as he twisted her arms behind her back like a pretzel and slapped his silver-plated cuffs onto her wrists, "I am placing you under arrest for the cold-blooded murder of Samantha Sterling. Anything you say can and will be used against you in a court of law, so I'd advise you to keep your lying trap shut!"

"Mr. Sterling! Mr. Sterling!" Mrs. Barnes' tears were streaming as she rushed into her own, precious kitchen. "Are you alright, son? Are you alright?"

"I'm okay, Mrs. Barnes," Sam said as he came to himself. His own hurt and rage had nearly taken him over the edge. "I'm much better...now...much better."

"Well, Chief Outlaw had one of his men blue-light me and pull my car over as I was leaving outta here this morning," Mrs. Barnes explained. "They took me to a safe spot until they were able to catch this witch red-handed. I told you she wasn't no 'count. And good riddance to bad rubbish!"

"Grrrr!! Joy howled. She was kicking and punching in her red-bottom stilettos and hurling obscenities at the top of her lungs. Her tears were flying like spitballs, and her face had puffed up like a chipmunk's. Her pricy lashes had come unglued, and black mascara was snaking down her face like licorice twists. The four uniformed officers were having a serious fight on their hands as they struggled to heave her into the police van.

"Where's the pretty girl, now?" Mrs. Barnes jabbed as the band of officers finally managed to haul Joy away, feet first.

"So, you know the whole story?" Sam said as he snatched the earwig from his ear; unclipped the button camera from his shirt; and stripped off the electronic listening device that had been taped to his chest. "Ouch...glad to get rid of all of these police gadgets—"

"Yeah, the officer told me most of what happened," Mrs. Barnes said. "I'm just ashamed that I didn't trust your judgement, Sam. I shoulda trusted that you know'd what you was doing." She giggled. "You always do."

"I'm just sorry I couldn't tell you all the sordid details myself, Mrs. Barnes." A reluctant smile teased at the corners of Sam's mouth. "But knowing how you felt about Joy, we figured your face would give our little scheme away—"

"So, do you think by Chief Outlaw listening in on what Joy had to say that he's got enough to convict her of murder? Lord knows she deserves it!"

"Well, the chief was recording our conversation, and his tape, along with the scientific evidence of Samantha's autopsy, should be enough to send Joy away to prison for a very long time—"

"Good." Mrs. Barnes nodded. "That's what she deserves for what she did to our dear, sweet Samantha...but, all in all, it's still a cryin' shame—"

"What?"

"That girl coulda been any good thang she wanted. Why she have to go and do a low-down thang like this?"

"There's no way of knowing, Mrs. Barnes." Sam pinned her with his tired eyes. "But I hope one good thing has come out of this fiasco—"

"And what might that be?" Mrs. Barnes cocked her head to one side.

"I hope this means you're back home...back home for good—"

"Right back!" Mrs. Barnes said with a happy laugh. "Right back here where I belong. You always hear me saying you're like the son I never had...'cause point o' fact, Mr. Sterling...I really ain't never been married...but...but I did lose my one-and-only baby boy...in childbirth. And I've been holding on to this family secret all these years...'cause I...I was so ashamed—"

"A-w-w, Mrs. Barnes, come here—" Sam said, and he grabbed her and hugged her tight enough to squeeze away all the pain and sorrow from their past. And for the first time since he'd lost his beloved Samantha, Sam broke down into cleansing tears in the arms of the woman he'd come to love and respect as a mother. "I am your family, Mrs. Barnes...and I'm grateful to you...grateful to you for everything!"

"Sam, I was surprised to get your call," Hope said as they were being seated in a quiet corner booth at a swanky bistro that was near the Riverwalk in Kansas City, Missouri. She'd dressed-up for the occasion. Her short 'fro was on point, and she was wearing a lovely, coral sheath that accentuated all of her luscious curves.

"I told you my business would bring me to Kansas City," Sam said as his handsome eyes washed over Hope admiringly. He was decked out in a blue silk shirt—opened at the collar—and the color caught the light in his rich, hazel eyes. And despite the rigors of his gut-wrenching ordeal, Sam looked no worse for the wear. In fact, if anything, it had heightened his rugged good looks.

"Yes, you said you'd call, but—"

"I wanted to see you, Hope," Sam admitted. "And…I would've come sooner, but I knew you needed time—"

"But—" Hope's eyes flickered as she recognized the sincerity of Sam's intentions. "But I thought…after everything…with Joy and all…I thought you'd never want to see me or my family ever again."

"Hope, I know you had nothing to do with what Joy did—"

"I know, but Joy…Joy's my twin cousin—"

"About that—"

"And I've tried to see her in that place…time and time again. But she won't see me, Sam. She won't even talk to me—"

"So, you don't know; do you?"

"Know what?"

"Well, you see, Joy is serving a mandatory life sentence in the Georgia State Petitionary for cutting my wife's life short." Sam's jaws tensed. "But when they opened the books on her past clients, they also found that Joy had caused the death of a least two more of her patients in two other states; and the investigation is still ongoing to uncover more potential victims—"

"Wh-at?" Hope shuttered; her back slumped against the booth.

"Yes, there are two confirmed cases...one in Maryland and one in Illinois," Sam explained. "So, even if Joy got paroled from her life sentence in Georgia...for whatever reason...the other two states are standing in line to prosecute her on their murder charges as well—"

"So...Joy will never get out of prison—"

"Never!" Sam nodded. "Joy will serve out the rest of her days where she belongs...locked up behind bars."

"Oh, Sam, I am so sorry," Hope said, trying not to tear up in the restaurant. "I feel so responsible for what Joy did to your wife...and to you. I don't know what happened to her. Growing up together, we were like two peas in a pod—"

"I've heard you say that before," Sam said compassionately, "but even two peas in the same pod are very different. No two things are exactly alike in this world. And even in our families, each of us is different...unique...one of a kind—"

"I know, but Joy and I were so close. We even joined church and got baptized on the same Sunday—"

"And exactly whose idea was that?" Sam's forehead creased.

"Well, the Sunday I felt called to go to the altar and get saved, I offered my hand to Joy...and like always...she accepted it. And we went up to the preacher together."

"Oh, I see. But coming to the Lord for salvation is an individual calling, Hope; it's not a team effort. The Lord already knows those who're His, and He does the calling—"

"Of course, you're right, but—"

"You were called, Hope; and, maybe, Joy just went along for the ride." Sam shrugged. "Ever think about that?"

"I just don't know." Hope sagged. "And I can't judge; but Joy is my one and only cousin, and I'm still praying for her—"

"And well you should," Sam said, "but just because you call her your *twin cousin*, or friend, or family, doesn't mean you're joined at the hip. You never were. You've made your choices, and she's made hers. And her choices have had dire consequences for which you are not responsible—"

"But I thought Joy and I were together…on everything—"

"You were in the same space; you both shared some of the same experiences; but you were not in the same lane." Sam gave his head a slow shake. "Who could've ever known that Joy had such an ugly heart?"

"I think her mother knew." Hope's voice hollowed. "Her mother often expressed concern about Joy's strange behavior, but no one took her seriously. But why would they? Joy was always…*the pretty one*—"

"Not to me." Sam said swiftly as his eyes washed over Hope's gentle face and her big, brown orbs.

"Oh, Sam, you're just saying that," Hope said, attempting to deflect his obvious compliment.

"And I mean what I say." Sam doubled-down. "But you're right about one thing. Mothers certainly do know their own children—"

"And Joy and I even went to the same college together…but I messed that up—"

"How so?"

"I…I overreacted to a boy's advances. I made a big scene about it. Later, I was so embarrassed that I ran back home for cover."

"Ever ask yourself why?"

"Oh, I know exactly why." Hope's breath thickened. "My Uncle Jude…the one I buried in Atlanta. Well…he…he tried to—"

"Molest you?"

"Yes…when I was very young." Hope's cheeks blazed hot with embarrassment.

"Welp…I guess every family tree holds secrets—"

"And when that boy pinned me down on that bed at college…I felt the exact same way Uncle Jude had made me feel. I couldn't breathe. I felt so small, so weak, so unloved…so ugly—"

"So, you came back home to Kansas City and left Joy to finish college alone?"

"Yes, and Joy has never forgiven me for being such a coward—"

"Maybe, it wasn't about finishing college, Hope," Sam said as he dismissed the attentive waiter with a gracious smile. He'd already made prior arrangements with the maître d' to reserve their table for the entire evening. "Maybe, it was more about you following your own calling—"

"But I should've finished what I started—"

"Joy finished college with flying colors…and what good did it do her?"

"Oh, Sam, I just don't know where Joy took a bad turn. But, maybe, if I'd stayed with her back then, things would be different—"

"No, Hope!" Sam firmed. "You need to get that notion out of your head. You need to stop seeing yourself in Joy's shadow. No matter what mind games she's played on you in the past, you are in no way responsible for her actions, anyone's actions, except your own—"

"I guess you're right." Hope relented.

"Of course, I'm right. The way we choose to live our lives matters. The Lord allows each of us to invest our talents in good things or bury them in bad. There're only two choices…God's way, or the world's way. We get to choose…but we also get to reap what we sow."

"So, I guess my twin cousin made her own choices—"

"Yes, she did, and you were never part of the equation," Sam said. "Joy's probably always been like this. It just took time for it to manifest itself…for her to grow into the fulness of her own ways. Remember what the Bible says?"

"What?"

"On the Lord's day, there'll be two in the same bed, and one will be raptured and the other left behind. So, no matter how much we're alike; no matter how our circumstances overlap; on that great day, we'll be separated by what we believe in our own hearts—"

"And there's no getting around that; is there?"

"No, Hope—"

"But I guess what Uncle Jude did...making me feel so weak and insignificant...it did make me work harder when I got back home. And since I've been back home, I've been able to build a thriving business and take good care of my parents who really do need me."

"Yes, you've flourished here." Sam smiled an admiring smile. "I'll have to be honest; I did take a sneak peek at your fabulous business enterprise. So, even the so-called bad stuff was actually guiding you into the Lord's plan for your life—"

"But how can you be so sure?"

"Oh, I know, Hope." Sam's voice dropped to a near whisper. "I know...because it happened to me. You see...I'm adopted—"

"What? You?"

"Yes, Hope—"

"But Joy thought—"

"Things are not always what they seem." Sam's jaws tensed, and his eyes swept the floor. "And, sure, Joy might've painted me into her own delusions of grandeur. But my only claim to fame is that the Lord has been good to me."

"So, you're adopted—"

"Yes, Hope, I'm adopted," Sam repeated, gauging her reaction. "And no one ever knew my family secret either...except Samantha."

"And, now, you're telling me?"

"Yes, I think you need to know. I think you and I have a lot in common." Sam nodded. "And I know I can trust you—"

"Of course, you can—"

"You see—" Sam pushed back into the booth and allowed his mind to reframe the memories he'd managed to dismantle. "When I was about four years old, my birth mother left me on the doorstep of a police station with a note pinned to my chest—"

"A note?"

"Yes." Sam's eyes strained up to the ceiling. "The note read: 'This is Sam. I tried. I can't. Your turn.'"

"And did they try to find them…your parents, I mean?"

"It wasn't possible." Sam shrugged. "I didn't know my birth father…and I called my birth mother only by her nickname, *Sparkle*. I didn't even know my own last name."

"Wow—"

"But my adoptive parents were a perfect fit for me, especially my new mother. She introduced me to Jesus. And when she died, her two sons by birth…my older adoptive brothers…they could never understand why I took it so hard. But the love and attention they'd taken for granted, I'd learned to cherish. What they squandered by living unfruitful lives, I used as a springboard for my success. And seeing my adoptive dad stay the course with me in such a loving way after his wife's death…despite the miserable shambles his own sons were making of their lives…gave me the courage to hang in there, too."

"So, what did your brothers do…that is your adoptive brothers?"

"Well, sad to say, the eldest one is on death row for a murder he committed during an armed robbery—"

"Oh, no—"

"And the younger one is a gang-banging drug dealer in our old neighborhood." Sam's voice gave way to sadness. "I'm just glad our dad didn't live to see it—"

"That's so sad." Hope's kind eyes embraced Sam's pain.

"I tried to help them," Sam said, "I truly did. But my brothers never really cared for me, and Samantha had to help me see that. As she'd often say, 'Just let it all go, Sam, and see what sticks.'"

"And did you?"

"Yes, I finally did let go...and I've not heard from either of my brothers since...and I doubt I ever will—"

"Samantha was a wise woman—"

"Yes, she really was. She had a way of shining light on my blind spots to help me make sense of the obvious." Sam squinted his kind eyes into a comic scowl. "Because, sometimes, we all need a little help seeing the truth that's right before our eyes—"

"So...what truth are you trying to help me see?" Hope's dimple twinkled back at his impish expression.

"Well, if you really want to know—"

"Tell me! Tell me!"

"Hope, you've tied too much of your identity to this *twin-cousins* notion." Sam stretched his eyes convincingly. "And I think you've been tying your life to a bogus anchor that's gone...or, maybe, never existed—"

"But everyone called us the twin cousins—"

"Yes, and, maybe, the people back then simply coupled you together for their own convenience...you know, a novelty for their own amusement. And, maybe, Joy liked being labeled *the pretty one* to satisfy her need to feel superior to you—"

"Huh?"

"But, Hope, you're definitely not weak. Look at what you've accomplished—"

"But that's just work, Sam. I'm really, really good at work. It keeps me busy...I don't have to think—"

"Yes, but you're the one who did it—"

"Yes...with the help of the Lord." Hope offered him a brisk nod. "The Lord has kept me and helped me in ways I could've never imagined—"

"Right!" Sam pressed his point. "And your *twin cousin* was nowhere in sight. Jesus has been your true anchor all along...not Joy—"

"But, Sam, you don't understand; the roots run so deep. Joy and I were nearly born together. We share the same family tree; attended the same schools; had the same friends—"

"Had the same opportunities—"

"Yes, we did—"

"But, Hope, you made different choices, and those choices have made all the difference. Don't you see that?" Sam hammered. "You chose the Lord's way. Joy chose her own way—"

"I know, Sam." Hope's countenance wilted. "But don't you see? My love should've been strong enough to hold us together. I feel like such a failure—"

"You're not a failure, Hope! It's not your fault!" Sam's kind eyes plead with her for her understanding. "Your love is not redemptive. You can't change people; fix things; or hold things together. Only Jesus' love has that kind of power. You couldn't hold onto Joy…any more than I could hold onto Samantha—"

"But—"

"This is not on you, Hope." Sam pressed his point. "It was your intention to always remain true and loyal to Joy. But she never made that same commitment to you—"

"Oh, Sam." Hope shivered. "You must be right. Joy probably never loved me like I love her…because she really did show me her true colors when she came to Kansas City and saw my business for the first time—"

"What happened?"

"I don't know." Hope shrugged. "Maybe…she couldn't stand seeing my accomplishments. She was supposed to stay two weeks and help me with my parents, but she stormed out after two days—"

"You wanted to give Joy love. Joy wanted to be better than you. It's not the same—"

"Is that why everything about me seemed to irritate her; nothing I did seemed to please her?"

"Probably—"

"But you don't understand, Sam! I would've given her anything I possess! Anything! I would've done anything in the whole world for Joy—"

"I know, Hope, but it didn't matter. She didn't want that. She might've been able to accept it from someone else, but she could never accept it from you. Don't you see?" Sam's warm, hazel eyes implored. "She liked thinking of you as the underdog, and she couldn't stand seeing firsthand that you're not...and you've never been. She wanted to stay just close enough to keep tabs on you, but not close enough to care about you—"

"And when Joy showed me how much she despises me...oh, Sam, she ripped my heart out!" Hope gasped for air like she was drowning in an ocean of disillusionment. "It's like everything I'd counted on...had ever felt sure of...crumbled right before my eyes. And if I've been so wrong about this for so long, how can I trust myself to be right about anything...ever again—" Hope's silent tears finally flooded her smooth cheeks despite her best efforts.

"Hope, I very much doubt Joy's capable of your kind of steadfast love," Sam said in a tone intended to sooth her. "Love is the Spirit of Christ, and people cannot give you what they do not possess—"

"But you don't understand, Sam." Hope sniffed. "Joy's contempt broke me down to my very core. I felt so betrayed...so rejected...so all alone—" She confided in an impassioned whisper. "I just wanted to disappear...to let go...to be no more—"

"Oh, Hope, you've loved the idea of Joy loving you for so long," Sam said, aching for her tears. "You've been wanting her to validate you...instead of learning to love yourself. But don't you see, Hope? This was not intended to break you down; it was intended to break you free...free of all of your misconceptions...so you can finally see the truth more clearly. And, now, it's time for you to let it all go—"

"But—"

"You had Joy imbedded so deep inside your heart. That's why it hurt so badly when she turned on you. But nobody belongs *inside* your heart, except Jesus," Sam said. "Pastor Jamie tells us that all the time—"

"So, Sam, what do I do?"

"Release Joy from your heart. Stop trying to make her be who she's not—"

"But how, Sam? How?"

"Let go of all of your expectations. See Joy for who she really is…not who you want her to be. And trust God—"

"But I failed God—"

"You can't fail God! You're a believer, Hope. You live in Jesus. You live in victory. You live in love. Jesus is on your side—"

"Then, that must be it, Sam! That's gotta be it!" Hope's eyes registered her delight. "Jesus did it!"

"Did what? What?"

"He knew how I felt about Joy." Hope's excited words spilled over. "He knew how Joy felt about me, and He wanted me to know, too. He wanted me to see that He has been my one-and-only source all of my life…not Joy…never Joy." Hope stiffened her back against the booth and spoke quietly as though she were communing with her own soul. "Yes, I can love Joy, but she can't live in my heart…not anymore. I can't hurt for her…not anymore. I can't let her bitterness hurt me…not anymore. Joy's life didn't turn out the way she planned it…but it is not my fault!"

"Now, you've got it, Pretty One!" Sam's smile broadened. He treasured seeing the renewed fire in Hope's eyes and the sparkle in her left cheek. "You can't make anybody love you; no matter what you do; no matter how hard you try—"

"Oh, Sam!" Hope shuttered. "I know…you're right…you're right about everything. But it's still so hard to let go of how I wanted things to be; how I expected things to be; and to accept the truth—"

"But don't you see, Hope," Sam said pointedly, "looking the truth straight in the eye can't hurt us anymore. In fact, all the ones who've let us down might've done us one, giant favor—"

"How so?"

"My birth mother's heartless actions drove me into the arms of Jesus; and, maybe, your Uncle Jude's evil actions did the same for you. They might've done it to hurt us, but they were fulfilling what we needed in our lives...a closer walk with our Saviour. And, yes, their actions were callous, and cruel, and mean, but they were also a blessing in disguise—"

"Oh, I see—"

"And that's why I can see my birth mother's failures as her failures, not mine. And you can see your Uncle Jude's failings...and Joy's failings...as their failings...not yours—"

"Oh, my—"

"And those feelings of being small, and helpless, and weak are just that...feelings. They were based on your uncle's lie, but they can be exchanged for new feelings based on God's truth."

"But how?" Hope looked deeply into Sam's hazel eyes.

"Faith cometh by hearing—"

"And hearing by the word of God," Hope said, completing the verse.

"Well, then, you do read your Bible." Sam teased. "I just needed to know—"

"Of course—"

"So, Uncle Jude said you were small and insignificant, but God's word says, 'You are complete in Christ Jesus.' Right?" Sam raised his brows. "Uncle Jude said you were unloved and ugly, but God says, 'You are accepted in the Beloved.'" Sam pressed his kind eyes into Hope's bright, brown orbs. "So...who're you gonna believe?"

"Oh, my!" Hope's wilted countenance blossomed afresh. "I'm going to believe God!"

"Right answer!" Sam cheered. "Because His word is much more important than what my birth mother did or your uncle did...or even what Joy did. God is bigger than any wrong you could do or any wrong that could be done to you."

"But Joy made me feel...so deserted...so naked—"

"How people treat you must be kept on the outside of your shield of faith...with only you and Jesus rockin' on the inside," Sam said with a chuckle. "At least, that's how Pastor Jamie puts it. He taught us that we're clothed in Christ...in fact, every piece of our whole armor is Jesus Christ, Himself—"

"I can see that!" Hope nodded as she mulled over the pieces of God's armor aloud. "He is my salvation...my righteousness...my peace...my truth...my faith—"

"Yep, all of it is Jesus!" Sam drilled her with his eyes. "So, whether people love you, or not, becomes a very small matter in the bigger scheme of things, huh? In Jesus, alone, we have everything we'll ever need to live this life. We are complete and whole in Him...regardless of what anybody else may say or do—"

"You're right!"

"We can't stop trouble, Hope, but we can rest assured that the Lord will be right there with us in it...if we trust Him—"

"So, I guess I just need to get over these bad feelings, huh?"

"No. Feelings are real." Sam's hazel eyes softened to a mellow hue. "And Jesus understands every hurt we could ever feel in this world. He lived here once, too; remember? And He suffered more than we could ever imagine. But, like Him, we have to operate on what God says rather than on how we feel. Our feelings have to be addressed...and if necessary, dismissed...by our unwavering faith in the Word of God."

"So, my faith can fix all these bad feelings?"

"Sure. That's why we're here...to trust God and put His word into practice...in an environment that will challenge us every step of the way." Sam's smile blossomed. "So, whether its relationships...or people...or hurts...we have to give them all over to the Lord. And when all of this is passed and gone...these mean people, these hard times, these heartaches, these tribulations, these losses...we'll have eternity to spend with our loving Lord—"

"So…is it my own pride that's making me hang onto these bad feelings…instead of taking God at His word?"

"Bingo!" Sam said, nearly clapping. "You've been mourning the life you wanted with Joy. But life is what it is…death is death…people are people…and we can't change that. We have to accept things as they come. So, it's time for you to lay your druthers aside, Hope, and face facts…no matter how harsh they may seem." Sam reached for Hope's hand, and she yielded it to his tender touch. "It's time for you to forgive your uncle. He was obviously struggling with his own demons. And it's also time for you to forgive yourself for allowing him to hold you captive all these years. That's over with. That's in the distant past." Sam squeezed her hand lovingly. "And you can also release Joy's hold over your life, too. You're not *twin* cousins. You're two, separate individuals with two, separate lives to lead—"

"Oh, Sam, thank you so much for helping me see things more clearly—"

"I wouldn't be talking to you like this if I didn't care, Hope." Sam's loving eyes burned into hers. "I am very attracted to you. But, first, I had to be sure that I could touch you…touch you with my heart…and touch your heart with the man that I am—"

"Oh, Sam—" Hope blushed, and her pretty smile set-off that lone dimple in her left cheek. "I just needed to know you're okay—"

"Hope, you just don't know how happy it makes me feel to see you smile again." Sam paused to enjoy the sheer beauty of it and to watch her dimple light-up the whole room. He adored the gentleness that graced her face, and he knew he would never tire of gazing into those big, mahogany eyes.

Quietly, Hope extended her other hand to Sam and said, "Can we pray about this?"

"We most certainly can." Sam held onto both of her hands firmly and tenderly. "'Cause I do love myself some praying women!" And Sam led them both in a fervent prayer; releasing their ties to the past;

forgiving the pain it had caused; and wiping everyone's slate clean—once and for all. And when the prayer was concluded, they sealed it in agreement, "In Jesus' Name, Amen."

"Now," Sam said, releasing one of Hope's hand and holding firmly onto the other, "can we talk about us?"

"Us?" Hope blushed as her heart raced with anticipation. She could no longer deny the seriousness of his intentions.

"Yes, Hope...us." Sam caressed her with his eyes. "The best thing Joy ever did for me was to bring you into my home for just one night. You came to see Joy, but I was glad to see you. And I thought...I was afraid...I'd never see you again...but I knew I would always want to—"

"But, Sam—"

"And I was glad that Mrs. Barnes invited you to the funeral. It was a blessing to me like you'll never understand." He smiled at the recollection. "Your presence was like a warm, fresh breeze—"

"Yes...Mrs. Barnes is a sweetheart—"

"Yes, she is—"

"And Pastor Jamie?" Hope said, making every attempt to redirect the conversation.

"Oh, he's fine and dandy, too." Sam chuckled. "He was able to maintain the church's upgrades...in spite of Joy's roadblocks...and the Soup Kitchen renovations are almost complete—"

"That's great—"

"Yes, and we can't wait for our visitors to not only experience the kindness of Christ through the food He provides, but to also be exposed to Him through His word...because everything we do at His church, we do in His name. We're trying to make disciples, Hope, just like He told us to—"

"And I know Samantha would be so pleased."

"Yes, that was Samantha's fondest dream...and it's just about to come true."

"That's marvelous!" Hope's eyes beamed.

"There you go again," Sam said, "lighting up my heart—"

"So, what else is going on in Sandywood?" Hope fidgeted with her napkin.

"Good try, Hope." Sam chuckled. "I see you, but I didn't come here to talk about Sandywood. I came here to talk about you...and me—"

"But, Sam...you love Samantha—"

"Yes, I love Samantha. I will always love Samantha. Love will never die." Sam's smile softened at her sweet remembrance. "But Samantha was a whole woman in Christ. I was not her anchor, and she was not mine. We both firmly believed that marriage bonds are extinguished upon death because that's the Lord's way. And that's why we fought so very hard to hold onto her life—"

"And Joy robbed you of that—"

"And I've forgiven Joy. I'm not looking for anyone to blame." The hard words croaked in Sam's throat. "Didn't you hear me in our prayer?"

"I did—"

"I was able to forgive Joy because I believe...despite her evil actions...I believe the Lord meant it for Samantha's good." Sam breathed. "Her body was failing. She only had a few weeks to live. And this...this may have been His way of sparing her any more pain, any more misery...any more agony—"

"Oh, I see—"

"But when we graduate to heaven, Hope, we no longer need these earthly bonds...all of our human connections are severed...our birthdays cease...our time here is completed. This life is made for the living, and marriage is for the here and now. But when we're in the presence of the Lamb, none of this will matter—"

"But how are you able to let go so easily—"

"Easy? It's not easy. Don't you ever think it's easy." Sam shook his head deliberately. "But we do not have the power to sustain things. That's the Lord's domain…and His alone. He gives each of us the people He wants us to have in our lives…for a season—"

"So, I guess it's us, then. We're the ones who try so hard to hold onto people and things and make them last a lifetime." Hope teared. "But everything and everybody is fading and passing away…except the Lord—"

"That's just the way it is, Hope. And as much as we might want to hold onto those who're gone, we can't. We can only love them and enjoy them while they're here; and when it ends, we must let go." Sam drew his trembling lips into a smile. "Releasing our loved ones…no matter how bad it hurts…is our way of honoring their memory and showing God that we accept His perfect will in the matter—"

"Yes, some things from our past don't survive…but we have to press on with the things that do…joyfully and thankfully—"

"Yes, Hope," Sam agreed. "The past is over and done. Each new day the Lord gives us is *Day-One*—"

"But, sometimes, people stop loving God…when things don't go their way—"

"True," Sam whispered, "and they get stuck looking back like Lot's wife—"

"And their hearts turn to stone—"

"But that's not us, right?"

"That can never be us—"

"We must move forward—"

"Our faith in the Lord demands it—"

"And the Lord will always be our first love—"

"Yes, indeed…no matter what!" Hope's conviction firmed, and her dimple danced.

"So, now—" Sam's eyes melded with hers, pleasantly content in their shared agreement. "Since you've stopped measuring your life by your past, your broken dreams, and the failures of others…over which you have absolutely no control…is it at all possible for you to start seeing your present reality as far better than you could've ever imagined?"

"How so?" Hope giggled freely at the playful twinkle in Sam's handsome eyes.

"Because now…your future could include me…us…together… in the here and now—"

"But, Sam…why me?"

"Because a man pursues what he wants—"

"But, Sam—"

"No more *buts*, Hope." Sam squeezed her hand tenderly; and, then, he released it. "I'll leave it right there. We'll relax and enjoy our meal. And I'll give you some time to contemplate the idea…the sweet possibility…of us…you and me…together…until we meet again."

****

"Call upon Me, and I will answer thee,
and show thee great and mighty things,
which thou knowest not."
~Jeremiah 33:3

Other Books by the Author
JEANETTA BRITT

Exciting Fiction
Pickin' Ground (The Lottie Series—Book One)
In Due Season (The Lottie Series—Book Two)
Lottie (The Lottie Series—Book Three)
Empty Envelope
W.O.O.F (Women of Overcoming Faith)
Living in the Seventh Day
Dipped in the Fire (The Fire Series—Book One)
Double-Dipped in the Fire (The Fire Series—Book Two)
Girl with the Mismatched Eyes
The Twin Cousins

Inspiring Poetry
Glimpses (poems of praise)
The Collection (poems of praise)
Flittin' & Flyin' (poems on death, birth & life)
Under the Influence—Spoken Praise
Poems From the Fast
Reunion
Third Ear

Join Jeanetta online:
www.jbrittbooks.com
www.Facebok.com/Jeanetta Britt
www.Facebok.com/JBrittBooks
www.Twitter.com/@JBrittBooks
www.Amazon.com/Jeanetta Britt
www.bn.com/Jeanetta Britt

****

*"For whosoever shall call upon
the name of the Lord shall be saved."*
~Romans 10:13

ABOUT THE AUTHOR

Jeanetta Britt is a bestselling author who graduated with honors from Fisk University and The University of Michigan. Her passion for writing action-packed Christian Fiction novels—filled with lots of juicy drama and suspense—as well as, Gospel poetry, surfaced over twenty years ago and has grown steadily ever since. "While being swept up in an exciting story," Jeanetta says, "I want my readers to *feel* the love of Jesus and take refuge in Him, like I did."

After completing a rewarding career in public administration in Dallas, Texas, Jeanetta returned to her native Alabama to write and to live. Her southern roots are reflected in her strong imagery, memorable characters, and delightfully witty storytelling style. She is a sought-after inspirational speaker, by youth and adults alike, with ten novels and seven books of poetry to her credit. When praised for her writing, Jeanetta often says, "Sometimes, I can't find the words, but they find me. I just have to be available—present—to write them down. More than a writer, I am a scribe."

Jeanetta is also an avid gardener and community advocate, and she founded Twelve Stones CDC—a non-profit organization that operates two community gardens in rural Alabama. "We provide free, fresh food for our community and an opportunity for our youth and senior citizens to form vital intergenerational connections, and to get some free exercise, companionship and sunshine, too," she says. "No rules—just love!"